MEN WOMEN AND CHILDREN

Alan Sillitoe

A STAR BOOK

published by

W. H. ALLEN

A Star Book
Published in 1975
by W. H. Allen & Co. Ltd.
A division of Howard & Wyndham Ltd.
44, Hill Street, London W1X 8LB

First published in Great Britain by
W. H. Allen & Co. Ltd. 1973

Printed in Great Britain by
Richard Clay (The Chaucer Press), Ltd., Bungay, Suffolk

ISBN 0 352 30094 9

These stories have appeared in:

Encounter
Nova
Morning Star
Penthouse
Winter's Tales

CONTENTS

AUTHOR'S NOTE

The nine stories in this book are those which I have decided to keep since the publication of my last collection five years ago. They are not printed in the order in which they came, but in the way I think best suited to their subject and mood.

The first story written was *Before Snow Comes*, in October of 1967. The last was *Chiker*, in the summer of 1972. But it is impossible to say when any of them were 'conceived' – as it is sometimes quaintly put. I like to think that my stories are drawn out, taken apart, rearranged, scraped, and polished. I can't say they were 'conceived' unless I have some idea as to who was responsible for the conception.

The first few pages of *Chiker* were written somewhat hastily about ten years ago, but were then put aside because I was not able to go on with it. I had drawn the portrait of the man, but did not know what to do with him. This only goes to show, I suppose, that my mind, if not my pen, is working at least ten years on every book of stories I publish. The same can also be said of my novels.

But the problems I associate with short stories are essentially poetic problems. If the inspiration comes which prompts me to start writing, and then for no reason stops abruptly, it is no good going on like a penny-a-liner to force an ending. I must wait, even as long as a decade, for the second inspiration which will allow me to finish it.

Some stories in the present book were begun and completed in this way, including *The View*, and *Scenes From the Life of Margaret*, and *The Chiker*, while others came out more or less whole and in the relatively short time it takes to complete the several drafts.

It will be seen that, as in my other volumes of stories, they all deal with 'Nottingham' people. That is to say, I again use Nottingham and its county as my stage, though it is unnecessary to point out that the breadth of activity, of movement and suffering, is as intense and deep when undergone by the people on this stage as on any other.

Far from it being easy to operate within such a framework, it becomes an added discipline. Emotions have to be delineated in the minds of people who are not usually prone to describing them. The same emotions and feelings are of course felt by them as by more voluble and literate people. Right from the start my novels and stories have been written on this basis and no other.

Under such conditions a writer must span the rough as well as the sophisticated – which is another way of saying that style and language are all-important, though not so vital that they obscure the tale that is to be told.

The problems of the simple are the problems of the gods. Those complicated people who are less down to earth are in many ways easier to describe, or at least no more difficult. What one writes about is of course a matter of choice, and the fact that one has made a choice, instead of spreading too wide and trying to write about everything, indicates that one has approached the problem in a poetic manner.

A story deals fundamentally with one person, one basic incident, one state of mind which fate is about to give a vicious twist to. However, the possibilities of extension within these limits can be wide enough. In *Mimic* the hero (shall we call him?) never goes beyond his own mind, though he does indeed go out of a mind which has breadth enough to encompass his departure, or split – and wait patiently for his return.

People nearly always triumph over incident, that is to say, over that malignant twist of fate. Otherwise there are only two alternatives – madness, or death. Death is a door that a writer can never break down, except in whimsy or fantasy, which show us nothing. Madness can be described and used as part of the story if the stricken person is to come out of it. But this can be such a long process that it usually has little place in a short story. Otherwise people are not defeated by circumstances, no matter how adverse or desperate. I have tried to show this with Margaret and her life, in the story which has her name in the title.

In *Pit Strike* the actual industrial lay-off figures large, but the story concerns Joshua, a Nottinghamshire coal-miner who reads nothing but the Old Testament. The story is about the fate of both Man and Book, and the strike is a background against which the man partially rediscovers himself.

Individuals are, therefore, the mainstays of these stories, not themes, or incidents, or messages of any kind except (though it is hardly necessary to state this) that people who live and suffer make up the sum totality of anything worth writing about. The people in my stories have the same sufferings as kings and queens, but their daily problems are more fundamental and tormenting.

Their court is a street-corner or a slum or a housing estate. It is only this attitude and this approach that can try to show the dignity that is intrinsic to them, and get anywhere close to their problems. They are my characters and my people, and how far I succeed in doing what I am trying to do can only finally be judged by them.

MIMIC

PART ONE

I learned to mimic at an early age, probably at two or three when I sat in front of the fire and stared at the cat. A mimic has a long memory, fine hands, and a face he can't bear to look at in the mirror, unless he puts on somebody else's with such intensity that he cannot recognize himself there. His soul is his own, but he buries it deeply with many others because under such a mound it is finally safe. Eventually of course it is so far lost and gone that he is unable to get down to it when he wants to, but that is another matter, and finally unimportant when one knows that age and death will settle everything.

In the early days of infancy I did not know I was becoming a mimic. By all accounts I was such a handsome baby that when my mother pushed me through town in a pram men would stop to admire me and give her five shillings to buy me a new rattle. At least that was her story, though my memory is better than any story, for another line was that because she was so pretty they gave money to me as an excuse for getting off with her.

A still further version could be I was so rotten-faced and ugly they gave her money to show sympathy at her being loaded with such a terrible burden. Anyway, that's how she met her second husband, which only proves that mimics usually have pretty and wayward mothers, while they may be fair-to-ugly themselves. You can't be a mimic with a fine-featured face, but for the first few years must stare at the world and take nothing in so that your face stays flat and putty-coloured, with a button-nose, beehive-mouth, and burdock-chin that deflects what sunlight hopes to make your features more heavenly to the world.

While father was at work and my mother in the scullery I'd romp on the rug for a while, then settle down and look at the cat, a black tabby with a white spot between its ears. I'd stare right into its splinter eyes till it opened its great mouth and yawned. Then, facing it on all fours, I'd open my mouth as well, full of small new teeth, stretching the side skin as far as it would go. The way the cat looked at me I knew I was successful, and because of this it seemed as if I felt alive for the first time in my life. I'll never forget this strong impression. When I mimicked, the light went on, as if somebody had sneaked up behind and slyly lifted off the dark glasses I didn't have. Finally the cat walked away, as if embarrassed.

I practised on animals for years, on the assumption, rightly I think, that if I could mimic animals so that they recognized themselves in me when I was doing it in front of them, then it would be quite easy to do it to human beings when I was ready for the changeover.

I remember at the age of nine that a young woman in our yard had a puppy, a small dark fat one that had been ill, that she wanted to get rid of. So she asked me to take it to the PDSA, gave me a shilling to put into their contribution box, and threepence to myself for the errand of taking it. The place was about a mile away, and going there I called in many sweet shops, buying chocolate at every stop. The puppy was wrapped in a towel in my arms, and after stocking up at a shop I would sit on a wall to eat the loot, and take another goz at the puppy who was going to be 'put to sleep' as the woman had said. I knew of course what that meant, and though the puppy squinted at me and licked my hand when I gave it chocolate it still looked as if it might welcome what was in store for it. I stared hard at those brown eyes, at that fat half-blind face that could never have any say in how the world was run, and between one snap of chocolate and the next I'd borrow its expression, take on that look, and show it to the puppy to let him feel he was not alone.

16

A mimic does what he is paid to do. By the time I got to the PDSA I had only threepence left for the contribution box. A shilling had gone on chocolate for me and the dog, and for the dog it was the last thing it would ever eat.

On the way home a hump-backed bridge crossed a canal. I went down through a gate on to the towpath. On the opposite side was a factory wall, but on my side was a fence and an elderberry bush. The water was bottle green, and reflected both sides in it. My eyes turned from grey to brown, and I barked as the dog had barked when the woman in the white overall had taken him from me.

This isn't a story about childhood. It is about a mimic, and mimics have no childhood. In fact it would almost be fair to say that they don't even have a life of their own. There is a certain price to pay for taking on another face, another voice, even though mimicry need bring no profit. But what mimicry does give is a continuation of one's life when for some reason that life had been forfeited even before birth. Whether one had done it oneself as a spirit from another age, or whether someone in another age had got hold of your spirit before it was born and squeezed the life out of it, who can ever be able to say? One may be born innocent, but in order to make one's mark on life, one has to get rid of that innocence.

One puts one's devilries as a mimic into other people if one is guilty of what blasted one's life before birth; one takes others' devilries upon oneself if one was innocent before birth.

To borrow a face is to show no mercy to it. In order to call it your own, you leave the owner of it with nothing. Not only do you see something of an advantage in using someone else's face, but you seek to rob them of what strength they also get from wearing it. At the same time you mimic them to hide yourself. A mimic therefore can't lose, except of course that he has lost everything before birth, more than anyone else can lose unless he is a mimic too.

17

The first *person* I mimicked, or tried to, was my mother, and I did this by falling in love with her. This is not so easy as it sounds, especially since she had been responsible for giving me birth, but being the person with the power of life and death over me there surely wasn't any fitter person to fall in love with. But I didn't let her see it, because my way of doing it was to mimic her one day, and I expected that since she had already given me so much she wouldn't mind this at all, would be flattered by it in fact. But all she saw was that I was taking everything.

She'd just had a blinding row with my father, and he'd stormed off to see his mates in the pub. At the heart-rending smash of the door behind him she sat by the fire waiting for the kettle to boil. When it did, she burst into tears. I thought to myself that if I did the same, her misery would be halved, so I put on the same expression (the half-closed eyes and twisted mouth, hands to my face-side with two fingers over my ear) and drew tears out with almost exactly the same noise. I'd meant to let my heart flow with hers, to be with it as a sort of comfort, but what I didn't know was that I'd only irritated her, mocked her – which is what she called mimicking for many years. This barefaced imitation made it worse, though instead of increasing her tears (it could hardly do that) it stopped them altogether. This was what I had hoped for, but only in such a way as to soften her heart, not to harden her. She smacked my face: 'Don't mock me, you little bleeder. You're almost as bad as he is.' I don't need to say who 'he' was, though in spite of our similarity he never became the mimic that I did.

So I mimicked my father, seeing how my attempt at love for mother had failed. It was quite a while before I stopped tormenting my mother by only mimicking my father in front of her, and began mimicking him to his face. When I did, he laughed, and I'd never seen him in such a good mood. Life is full of surprises for a mimic. He'd loosened his belt one

Sunday dinner because he was too full of beer and food. He pulled me on to his knee and kissed me, my mother looking wryly over her shoulder now and again as she washed the pots. He was so pleased at my exact imitation of him, of seeing himself so clearly in me, that he gave me a shilling.

This momentary gain went to my head and, before he could fall into a doze by the fire, I thought I would put on the best show he'd seen by mimicking my mother for him. If he could laugh at himself in me, he'd be more touched than ever to see mother in my face.

I drew myself up on the hearthrug as if I were tall and thin, curved my arms outward from my side, tilted my head, and drew in my cheeks, completely altering the shape of my mouth and putting that fire into my eyes that expected to be swamped out any second by a tidal wave.

'You've been a long time at the pub,' I said in her voice, 'don't you know your dinner's burnt? It's a wonder you couldn't smell it right from the bar.'

His eyes grew small, and the smile capsized like a boat in a gale. Before I knew where I was I was flat on my face. Then a boot got me in the ribs and I was curled up by the stairfoot floor.

Somehow, mimicking my mother in front of my father hadn't upset *her* at all, not like when I'd done it for her alone. In fact she was amused now, so when the old man lashed out at me with the old one-two of fist and boot, she cried and railed in my defence, calling him all the cruel gets under the sun.

'You leave my son alone,' she shouted, 'you drunken bully. I'll get the police in next time you kick him like that. He's never done any harm to a living soul, and you've never treated him right, either.'

Father was baffled. He'd not liked me being disrespectful, he said, as if he'd been at church instead of a pub. I hadn't any right to mock her. As for him, he could stand it because it was

19

only a bit of a joke, but he didn't like me doing it to her, the wife and mother of the house.

By this time I'd uncurled myself from the hedgehog position (I could imitate a hedgehog very well at times) and had seated myself at the table. I wasn't crying. A mimic soon learns to stop that sort of thing, otherwise he'd never do any mimicking at all. To get kicked was one of the risks you ran. And because I wasn't in tears, they soon made up their quarrel which, after all, had only started because of me. He put more coal on the fire, and she made him some fresh tea. When that was finished they talked and laughed, and she sat on his knee. Then they went upstairs together for a Sunday sleep, and I was left downstairs alone on the hearthrug wondering where I'd gone wrong. I didn't even have the energy to mimic a strong man booting the cat out of the way because things hadn't gone too well for him at work.

Some people believe that simplicity can only come out of madness, but who wants to go through madness in order to achieve the dubious advantage of becoming simple? Only a mimic can straddle these two states and so avoid being himself. That is to say, he finds a way of not searching for himself in order to avoid discovering that he has no self, and therefore does not exist. To see finally that there is nothing behind all the faces of one's existence is to find real madness. And what simplicity is there in that?

At school, I was the sort of person of whom the other boys asked: 'Is it going to rain today?' even though I looked nothing like a sage or weatherman. But the clouds or empty sky seemed to be on my side, and I was often right when I told them one thing or the other. It wasn't so much that I could guess the weather as that I'd take a chance on saying what I thought was going to happen. This comes easy to a mimic, because every person or object that he decides to imitate has a vein of risk in it.

In my young days it took a long while for me to realize that whenever I decided to mimic someone, and actually went through the process of doing so, I was filled with a deep interest in life and did no harm to anybody. But in between times I was remote and restless in turn, and liable to delve into all kinds of mischief. If I was not inspired for weeks to mimic, and at the same time found no opportunity otherwise to work off my bilious spirit by getting into trouble, then I took ill with some current letdown of the body such as pneumonia or mumps. My father and mother would have liked to have blasted me for the bother I gave them but after I had mimicked them successfully so early on they went out of my life for ever in any important way, and I took so little notice of their rage against me that many people and other members of my family began to look on me as a saint – until my next rampage.

One Christmas at school there was a fancy-dress party before breaking up for the holidays. I went as a moth, with two great wings and white powder all over me. Some came as musketeers and spacemen, but most appeared as nothing at all, simply wearing a badge, or hat. It was an old school, but there was a stage at one end of a big classroom. I received first prize, somebody else got second, and another boy third. The other two were told to get on the stage and act out what they were supposed to be. They did their best, then I went up.

A teacher put a candle on a low table, and I became a moth, weaving around it so that everybody stopped talking and looked. Maybe the teachers told them to be quiet. It was raining in the street, and perhaps being out of it and in the warmth made it easier for me to mimic a moth, with two wings and dry powder all over me. I went round and round the candle, my eyes half closed, and the flame hardly moving. I took the moth into me, and later heard that they began to laugh. I must have known this, yet didn't know it, at the time. But I went on circling the candle, and nobody thought to stop me, to break my spell and their spell.

If life is one long quest to avoid deciding what you are, I suddenly knew that I was a moth when one whole wing was touched off by the candle.

The flame came up suddenly and without smoke, but it wasn't as swift to others as it was to me, and before more than a slight scorch was done the flame was killed stone dead by two of the teachers.

Everybody thought that my days of mimicking were done for good. So did I, because on that occasion it seemed to have got out of control, and though I thought I might like such a thing to happen at some time in my life, I wasn't ready for it yet.

Before leaving that part of my life for ever (I still can't bring myself to call it childhood) I remember a photograph of me, that showed a big self-absorbed boy of thirteen. It was taken by an uncle, and then enlarged, and my mother had it framed and put on the sideboard in the parlour where nobody went and so hardly anybody, thank God, ever looked at it. I'd been out of her care and bother for a long time, but she'd taken to liking me again. It made no difference, because once a decision is taken through a failure to mimic, nothing can alter it. Maybe I reminded her of my father who had long since gone and given place to another person, and who she still in some way liked. But I'd never mimic him for her, even so, though I could have done it so that the house would have crowed around us.

This photo seemed to have no connection with me, but everybody swore that it had, and that there couldn't be a better one. In my heart I'd come to the age where I wanted to please them, so I decided I must mimic that photo so as to become like the image on it. It wasn't long before I saw that such a thing was not feasible. If you don't know what you are, how is it possible to imitate yourself? This was the issue that burned me. I could not imitate something that had no life, not

22

even myself if I didn't have any. And certainly judging by the photo there was no life there whatever. That was what everyone liked about it, my mother most of all, who stuck it on the sideboard in what was to her the place of honour.

Nevertheless, I looked at that photo for a long time, since other people had given it so much meaning. It was there for the world to see, above all, those who close their hearts and say: Know thyself. But I say: Get me a mirror, and according to the antics performed in it you can then (if you have that sort of desire) know everybody in the world.

But a photograph is not a mirror. You do not even see yourself as others see you. For a moment I almost went into the spirit of that photograph, but pulled myself back in time. That would have been evil. I preferred not to know what I was. There was almost triumph in that decision. If I don't know what I am, nobody can know, not even God. And if God doesn't know, then there is no God.

Rather than mimic the photograph of myself and believe in God I decided that I'd sooner be a moth.

Being such a good mimic I couldn't hold down any job for long. Sooner or later the foreman was bound to turn up when I was doing an imitation of him before all my mates. I worked harder than most though because I was so self-absorbed that nothing was too difficult or arduous for me. It was always with great regret that I was sacked.

On the other hand, all women love a mimic, except the mimic's mother, who ceases to matter by the time he becomes interested in other women. If you want to get off with a woman all you have to do is talk. Let the steamroller roll, and talk, talk, talk. Flatter her if you must, but the main thing is to talk. No woman can resist a constant stream of fulsome talk, no matter how inane and irrelevant, as long as you keep it up and make her laugh. Even if she laughs at you, it doesn't matter. By that time she's softening, you can bet.

And a mimic, even if he's so much speechless putty when left alone with himself, can mimic a funny and talkative man when the need arises. Of course, when the girl falls in love she never gets what she thinks she is getting. But then, who does? There is much wisdom in the world. Certain basic rules were formulated for me by Sam England who worked in the plywood factory where I took my first job. Never, he said, marry a girl who hates her mother, because sooner or later she will start to hate you. He also added that if you want to know what your girl friend is going to look like in thirty years' time, look at her mother now. And if you want to know what your girl-friend expects you to look like in *ten* years' time, look at her father.

Whenever I met a girl I had to decide, by her face and talk, and the sort of home she came from, what sort of a person she'd like me to be. There weren't many girls who could ever put up with a strong silent type for the first three dates while he weighed up the situation. But after that I fell into the slot, and the talk began, the endless jokes and self-revelations that come from anyone no matter what sort he is.

If I wanted to get rid of a girl, I made an abrupt change of character. None of them could stand this. They thought I had either gone mad, or lost my respect for them. In the soiled territory of the heart the precise configuration of the land only comes with continual and intense familiarity.

One girl I could not get rid of. I changed character no less than five times, but she wouldn't go away, so there was nothing I could do except marry her.

If there's one thing I've always found it hard to mimic it's a happy man. I've often been happy, but that was no help when I was indifferent and wanted to let someone else see that I was full of the joy of life. I knew that I had to overcome this problem and prayed that on this vital issue my talent for mimicry would not let me down.

In the very act of getting married, in order to appear happy to the girl I was to live with, I had to behave like a fool. When I should have slipped the ring on her finger I put it on mine – then on to hers. When we were declared married I attempted to kiss the best man, a fellow clerk from an office I was then working at. He fought free and pleaded with me not to be bloody silly, so then I kissed the bride, and apologized to everyone later by saying I'd been too happy to know what I was doing. They believed this, and forgave me, and I loved them so much I could have mimicked them all, one after another to the end of time.

When I changed for the sixth time it was only to mimic a man getting married. That was the one character she couldn't stand, and by the time I had come to believe in the act, and had almost grown to like it, it was the one finally by which I got rid of her. When we parted six months later I did a very tolerable job of mimicking an amicable man, who had taken one step wrong in life and wanted to go two steps back. She went home to her parents, and took the television set among all her cases in the second run of the taxi. We had always made love in the most perfect way, because I'd had enough experience to mimic that like a stallion, but it had made no difference to our final feeling for each other. She'd never been able to get through to the real me, no more than I had. And after a year of trying she imagined she never would, and I couldn't help but admire her promptitude in getting out as quickly as she did.

This is not a tale of love, or the wail of a broken marriage, or a moan about impossible human relationships. I won't dwell long on any of that. I can go on for years telling you what all this is *not*. It'll be up to you to tell me what it is.

Ambition has never been strong in my veins. To be ambitious you have first to know what you are. Either that, or you do not have to be concerned with what you are. My talent for mimicry was an end in itself. If I could observe someone, I thought in the early days, and then become exactly the same, why should I go through years of work to accomplish it in the reality of society?

I had never any intention of working, but what society demands of you is in fact what life itself wants. So you must imitate it – instead of allowing your soul to be destroyed by believing in it. As soon as you accept something, and cease to play a role regarding it, you are done for. Your soul is in danger. You have even less chance then of ever getting to know the real nature of yourself.

The same must be with everything you are called upon to do in life, whatever action, whether it lasts a minute or a year. Mimic it, I told myself at times of danger when caught by a suspicious joy of life I was about to aquiesce to. The successful mimic is he who not only takes on a role completely so that everyone is deceived, but actually from a distance sees himself with his own eyes doing it so that he himself is never deceived. I only learned to do this later, probably after I broke up with my first wife.

One might imagine that if the main thing in life was the survival of the fittest, then one as a mimic would be wise to imitate and continue to imitate one of the fittest. But not only would that be boring, it would be inhuman, and above all foolish. We know that it is not the fittest who survive, but the wise. The wise die, but the fittest perish, and they perish early on from having settled on to one role in life. They have determined to keep it to the very end, and also to defend it to the death against those who would try to show them that the world is richer than they have made it.

It is the easiest thing in the world for me to recognize those who believe in the survival of the fittest, which means most people. It is, conversely, difficult for me to meet another person like myself, because there are so few of us.

But I once met a woman who was also a mimic. What I could never understand was why those qualities that I had,

26

made people trust and love me, especially women. If to mimic is to betray (which it certainly is) then you would expect to be generally disliked, but strangely enough it was more often the opposite. She said exactly the same thing, except that it was especially men who loved and trusted her.

A friend of mine from the insurance office where I worked was getting married, and I met her at the reception for it. She was a thin green-eyed girl from the tobacco factory, and I listened to her during the meal mimicking the parson, for she had also been at the church. As a lesser friend of the bride's she was assigned to a more remote table, and I happened to be passing on my way back from the lavatory, where I had mimicked a disgusted man and thrown up what food I'd already eaten.

The people around her didn't know whether to be amused or offended. I was merely interested. Her face lost its pallor and grew weightier with the sombre voice she put on. She had great range of tone, and as she went through the service I took the part of bridegroom. Instead of saying 'I will,' at the correct moment, I said: 'I'm damned if I will,' and the two nearest tables joined in the applause.

The actual bride, as this went on, shook at the mouth and dropped tears on to her cheeks. The best man and the bridegroom demanded that we pack it in, but some devil was in us both, and our duet went on as if we were in the middle of a field with no audience at all. There was silence for a few minutes before the uproar. A pair of fine mimics had met, an accident of two stars clashing in interstellar space, and nothing could stop us getting to the end of the act.

The last word was with the best man. I suppose the bridegroom was saving himself for the first night. He only nodded in despair, knowing that it couldn't end in any other way. When the man hit me I pulled two chairs over and half dragged the tablecloth on to the floor. I sprang up and, mimicking an outraged partygoer whose best piece was being unjustly spat

27

on, punched him right over the table, where his head spliced down through the four-tier cake.

The bride screamed as if her husband had been killed. I'd had enough. Grabbing the slender fingers of my fellow mimic I ran out of that doom-laden party for all I was worth, wondering how long the marriage would last after such an inauspicious beginning.

Our association was interesting, but disastrous from the start. We didn't live together, but shared each other's rooms. For a few months it was champagne and roses. Coming back to one of the rooms from our respective jobs we would eat a supper (imitating each others mastication all the way through), then we would dare each other to mimic certain characters, such as an airline pilot, a policewoman, an insurance man, girl shop assistant. We played with each other, tested each other, acted God and the Devil with the deepest penetrable parts of our hearts and souls. We mimicked each other mimicking each other. We mimicked each other mimicking people we both knew. We mimicked the same person to see who could do it best. When we emptied each other we made love, and it came marvellously on such occasions. We thought we had come to the end of the road, gone over the cliff hand in hand like a couple of Gadarene swine and found we had landed in paradise.

But to think such things only means that the road is about to enter a swamp. I wanted her to marry me, but it turned out she was already married. So was I. Her husband knocked on my door one Sunday afternoon, and what could I do but ask him in? He was a van driver of thirty, but with his sweater and quiff he looked seventeen. He appeared stupid and sensitive, a not uncommon combination. 'I know you're living with him,' he said, 'but I've come to ask you to come back and live with me. That's why I've come.'

I stood up and made a quiff in my hair, threw off my jacket, and pulled the sweater down. Then I repeated his speech in exactly the same voice. It's dangerous mimicking simple people, but I couldn't resist. He must have gone through all the possible situations that could arise before he knocked at my door, but this wasn't one of them. He looked horror-struck, and leaned against the outside door. At this, Jean, who'd said nothing so far, got up and stretched her spine against the door to the kitchen with exactly the same expression.

'What's going on?' he demanded.

'What's going on?' I mimicked.

He lifted his fist as if about to fly through the room and crash against me. Jean lifted her fist and prepared to spring in exactly the same way. They would have collided and died in an apotheosis of glorious mimicry.

He turned to the door and opened it. Jean pulled at the kitchen door. We heard him running downstairs, and he never came back.

I passed him a few months later as I was walking through town. A girl was with him, and he didn't notice me in my misery. But I saw him all right because I hadn't seen anyone so obviously happy for a long time.

I followed Jean from the factory one night, and she met another man.

She'd been seeing me less and less. I'd expected it, but because we couldn't live together, could only exist like two cripples, taking turns to hold each other up, I was struck by jealousy as if a javelin thad shuddered deep between my shoulder blades.

When two vampires meet, they meet for ever, until another comes to set them free. But freedom is painful, for a while. For a mimic who doesn't believe in it, it can be catastrophic.

I rang the bell of his flat one Sunday morning. As he opened the door Jean made a good imitation of the ringing noise. I saw that I was in for a bad time. Think of what situation you want from the bottom of your soul to avoid, and when you have decided what it is, consider what you'll do when it comes about.

He was grinning by the window, and Jean actually offered me a cup of tea. While she was giving it to me I could see her imitating her actions. She had learned a lot, and I wondered where. I never knew his name. To the world he was an ordinary chap in some trade or other, but to me I saw he was trying to mimic something and I didn't know what it was. I was puzzled, but sat and drank my tea.

I asked Jean how she was, but she only smiled, and didn't seem to know. I wondered if she was happy, and could only say that she was. I knew that if I asked direct questions they would combine to defeat me in mimicry, and I had no wish to bring on to myself what Jean and I had poured on to her husband. They knew this. He stayed by the window, grinning, and I withered under the stare that went with it. Nevertheless I looked up at him from time to time. His face seemed a shade paler and thinner. I would fight on my own ground, in other words get up and go – but not before I could see what he was imitating.

But the stare grew ashen and luminous, especially after I had nothing left to say. I stood up and made for the door, but Jean blocked it. Where had she met such a person?

'I'm going,' I said calmly. A mimic cannot give up the ground he stands on, without knowing that another piece of land is waiting for him. Here, I was isolated, and the ocean was wide. It wasn't an honour to be defeated at this moment, but it was essential to me as a man. In defeat one can begin to know what one is, in victory – never. 'Get out of my way.'

Behind my back I heard: 'I'm going. Get out of my way' – in my own voice exactly.

'Guess what he's mimicking?' she said.

Without turning around I saw reflected in her eyes the sky-blue bones of his skull head, and the fixed grin of the victory I'd been forced to give him.

I mimicked her: 'Guess what he's mimicking?' and didn't give her time to answer. 'A corpse,' I said, forcing her gently aside, opening the door, and walking away.

Between bouts of mimicking one person and another, my entity becomes blank. To be able to mimic someone I had to like them. That was the first rule, just as, in the reverse sense, in order to love someone you have to be able to mimic them. When I mimicked people now, they ceased to like me, if they had ever done so. But then, treachery always begins with a kiss. For these reasons I had found it impossible to imitate God, and not only because I'd never seen Him.

Later, in my isolation, I only mimicked people to myself instead of out loud or for the benefit of others. Don't force the pace. This isn't a story. Switch off if you're not with me. I'll go on as long as you can, if not longer. I've had everything: booze, pot, shock, solitary. Yet though I may be sane, and a mimic of the world, can I imitate Mr Sand or Mr Water, Mr Cloud or Mr Sky with sufficient conviction to become all of them rolled into one realistic and convincing ball?

I mimic myself trying to mimic myself when I don't know who I am or what my real self is. I sit on my own in a pub laughing inwardly because I am more king of the world than anyone else. I see faces around me both troubled and serene, and don't know which one to choose for the great grand mimic of the night. I give up trying to mimic myself, and choose a man talking earnestly to his wife. I stand in the middle of the floor. Everything is clear and steady, but no one looks at me. I talk as if the man's wife were standing two inches from my face, grinning at the jokes I'm (he's) obviously making, then looking slow-eyed and glum when she mentions the children. Somebody pushes by with an empty glass as if I don't exist. I pull him back and he knocks me down. I do exist. I live, and smile on the floor before getting up. But only he notices me, and does so no more as his glass is filled and he steps by me

31

back to his table. It is quite a disturbance, but they don't even call the police.

Was Jean's new man mimicking himself, or was it me? I shall never know. But I would not see her again, even though she might want to take up with me. She'd been in contact with evil, and the evil had rubbed off on to her. Some of it in that short time had jumped to me, and I was already trying to fight free of it.

When I was mimicking someone I was walking parallel with the frontiers of madness. When I did it marvellously well, the greater was the drop of madness below me. But I didn't know this. I was driven to mimicry by threat and fear of madness. For some months I totally lost the skill to mimic, and that's why I got a note from my doctor and presented myself at the door of the local head-hospital. They welcomed me with open arms, and I was able to begin making notes from the seven millionth bed.

I did well there, announced to all assembled that I was now going to put on a show of mimicking Doctor So-and-so, and what to me was a brilliant act for them turned out to be perfectly still flesh and a blank stare from a person who was me in the middle of the room.

I had to start again, from the beginning. In order to imitate a sneeze I was thrown on to the floor by the force of it. I turned into a dog down one side of my face, and a moth on the other.

As I came up from the pit I started to write these notes. I have written them out five times already, and on each occasion they have been snatched from me by the attendant and burned. While I write I am quiet; when I stop, I rave. That is why they are taken from me.

PART TWO

I didn't stay long: it took me two years to recover. To imitate
was like learning to speak again. But my soul was filled with
iron, and I went on and on. The whole world was inside of me,
and on any stage I chose I performed my masterpiece of
mimicry. These were merely rehearsals for when I actually
figured as the same person over and over again, a calm,
precise, reasonable man who bore no relation to the real me
seething like a malt-vat inside. The select audience appreciated
my effort. I don't think anything was lost on them, except
perhaps the truth.

No one can mimic time and make it go away, as one can
sometimes make friends and enemies alike disappear when you
mimic them. I had to sit with time, feed it my bones in daylight
and darkness.

This great creation of mine, that I dredged up so painfully
from the bottom of my soul, was someone I'd sidestepped from
birth. I breathed life in him, a task as hard as if he were a stone,
yet I had to perfect him and make him live, because in the
looney bin I realized the trap I'd walked into.

I made a successful imitation of a sane man, and then they let
me out. It felt like the greatest day of my life. I do not think my
performance could have been better than it was.

An insane man can vanish like a fish in water, and hide anywhere. I am not insane, and it was never my intention to
become so. But one is forced to mimic to perfection a sane man
so as to become free, and what greater insanity is there than
that? Yet it widens the horizons of the heart, which is no bad
thing for someone who was born a mimic.

Years have passed, and in my pursuit and mimicry of sanity

I have become the assistant manager of a large office. I am thirty-five years of age, and never married again. I took some winter leave and went to Switzerland. Don't ask me why – that means you, the one I'm imitating, and you, who I am not. I planned the space off work and set off for London with my pocket full of traveller's cheques and a passport. In my rucksack was a hammock, nylon groundsheet, blanket, tobacco, matches, soap, toothpaste, toothbrush, compass, a book, notebook, and pencils. That's all. I don't remember where I got such a list from but I did, and stuck to it religiously. I was determined that every action from now on should have some meaning, just as in the past every time I had ever mimicked anyone had also had some important significance. One cannot live in the world of chance. If fate will not act for you, then take it by the neck.

It was so cold I thought my head would break like an old teapot, but as I walked away from the lake and along the narrow road between banks of trees I got used to it. The walls of the mountains on either side were so steep it seemed that if anybody were foolhardy enough to climb up they would fall off and down – unless they were a fly. Perhaps I could mimic a fly, since already in the cold I had conjured a burning stove into my belly. A car passed and offered me a lift. I waved it on.

It was getting dark by five, and there wasn't much snow to be seen, a large sheet of luminous basilisk blue overhead, and behind me to the south a map-patch of dying fluorescent pink. The air was pure, you could certainly say that for it. The sun must have given the valley an hour each day, then a last wink before it vanished on its way to America.

There was snow underfoot, at certain higher places off the road, good clean snow that you could eat with honey on it. I could not see such snow and fading sun without death coming into my heart, the off-white powder humps in the dusk thrown between rock and tree-boles, flecked among the grey and scattered rooftops of a village I was coming to.

Bells were sounding from the church, a leisurely mellow music coming across the snow, so welcoming that they made me think that maybe I had had a childhood after all. I walked up the steep narrow lanes, slipping on the snow hardened into beds of ice. No one was about, though lights were in the windows of dark wooden houses.

Along one lane was a larger building of plain brick, and I went inside for something to eat. A girl stood by the counter, and said good evening in Italian. I took off my pack and overcoat, and she pointed to tables set in the room behind.

They did not ask me what I wanted but brought soup, then roast meat, bread, and cabbage. I gave in my passport, intending to stay the night. A woman walked in, tall, blonde, rawboned, and blue-eyed. She sat at another table, and fed half her meal to the cat. After my long trek from the railway station (stopping only in the town to buy a map) I was starving, and had eyes for nothing but my food. The first part of the walk was agony. I creaked like an old man, but now, in spite of my exhaustion, I felt I could walk on through the night.

I did not sleep well. In dreams I began to feel myself leaving the world. My hand was small and made of copper, tiny (like hammers that broke toffee when I was a child), and I placed it on my head that was immense and made of concrete, solid, but that suddenly started to get smaller. This was beginning to be an actual physical state, so I opened my eyes to fight it off. If I didn't I saw myself being pressed and squeezed into extinction, out of the world. It didn't seem as if I would go mad (nothing is that simple) but that I would be killed by this attrition of total insecurity. It seemed as if the earth were about to turn into concrete and roll over my body.

I got out of bed and dressed. The air in the room, which had firmly shut double windows and radiators, was stifling. When you think you're going mad it's a sign you're getting over it. The faces of everyone I'd ever mimicked or made love to fell to pieces in turn like a breaking jigsaw puzzle.

My boots bit into the snow as I closed the door behind. It wasn't yet midnight. There was a distinct ring around the full and brilliant moon. There was snow on the mountain sides, and it seemed as if just over the line of their crests a neon light was shining. I walked along the lanes of the village, in the scorching frosty cold.

To question why one is alive means that one is only half a person, but to be a whole person is to be half dead.

Sun was shining over the snow next morning as I sat by the window drinking coffee. I was near the head of the valley, and the mountain slopes opened out. Most of it was sombre forest with occasional outcrops of rock, but to the west, at a place shone on directly by the sun, I could see green space. Then nothing but rock and snow, and blue sky. My eyes were always good. I never needed glasses or binoculars, and just above the meadow before the trees began was a small hut. No smoke came from it.

I paid my bill, collected my pack, and said good-bye. At the road a cow had been hit by a car and lay dying. The car's headlamp was shattered and the animal lay in a pool of blood, moving its hoofs slightly. A group of people stood around, and the driver was showing his papers. Another man rested a note-book on the car-top to write. It was all very orderly. I pushed through and looked into the eyes of the dying animal. It did not understand. As a last gesture it bellowed, but no one was interested in it, because the end was certain. No one even heard it, I was sure. The damson eyes were full of the non-comprehension of understanding.

The mountains were reflected in one, and the village in the other – or so it seemed as I paced back and forth. Another bellow sounded, even after it was dead, and when all the people looked at me at last to make sure that the noise was coming from me and not out of the sky I walked on alone up the road, away from the spoiled territory of the heart, and the soiled landscape of the soul.

I am wild. If I lift up my eyes to the hills a child cries. A child crying makes me sad. A baby crying puts me into a rage against it. I imagine everything. If I go into the hills and sit there, birds sing. They are made of frost, like the flowers. Insanity means freedom, nothing else. Tell me how to live and I'll be dangerous. If I find out for myself I'll die of boredom afterwards. When I look along the valley and then up it seems as if the sky is coming into land. The mountains look as tall as if they are about to walk over me. If they want to, let them. I shall not be afraid.

The wind is fresh except when it blows smoke into my face. I build a fire by the hut, boil water on it for tea. The wind is increasing, and I don't like the look of the weather.

The hut is sheltered, and when I came to it I found as if by instinct a key just under the roof. There's nothing inside, but the floor is clean, and I have my hammock as well as food. When it is dark it seems as if the wind has been moaning and prowling for days, plying its claws into every interstice of the nerves. I wanted to get out and go after it, climb the escarpment above the treeline with a knife between my teeth, and fight on the high plateau in the light of the moon, corner that diabolic wind and stab it to death, tip his carcass over the nearest cliff.

I cannot mimic either Jack Frost or a windkiller. It's too dark, pit-shadows surround me, but there's no fear because outside in the mountains the whole fresh world stretches, waiting for children like me to get up in the morning, to go out into it and be born again.

I have finished with mimicking. I always thought the time would come, but could never imagine when or where. I cannot get into anyone any more and mimic them. I am too far into myself at last, for better or worse, good or bad, till death do me part.

One man will go down into the daylight. In loneliness and darkness I am one man: a spark shot out of the blackest pitch of night and found its way to my centre.

A crowd of phantoms followed me up, and I collected them together in this black-aired hut, tamed them and tied them down, dogs, moths, mothers, and wives. Having arrived at the cliff-face of the present there's little else to say. When my store of food is finished I'll descend the mountainside and go back to the inn, where I'll think some more as I sit drinking coffee by the window, watching the snow or sunshine. I'll meet again the tall, blonde, rawboned, blue-eyed woman who fed half her meal to the cat – before setting off on my travels. Don't ask me where, or who with.

PIT STRIKE

As the long line of bodies bunched up at the centre and collided with the police a cry went out: 'Get your false teeth into his knackers, Joshua!'

It was a Welsh voice whose owner may not have seen Wales even as a child, having inherited the accent from the haven of his family. Many such militants at Aylesham had gone to the Kent coalmines when they had first opened forty years ago. Some had been blacklisted in Wales after the strike of 1926, and denied work in the place they belonged, while others went to Aylesham hoping for better rates and conditions.

The voice and its foul words enraged Joshua, who had come down from Nottinghamshire to help with picketing, but such was the force of men at his back that he was unable to turn round and get at it, there being nothing he could do with his anger except vent it on the red-faced policeman in front.

Perhaps the miners were beginning to get Joshua's number at last, by goading him in this way, for as he kicked and punched – keeping his hands low enough to be fairly hidden – he became calmer at realizing it was only a mark of solidarity after all. He was almost glad of the copper's kick aimed at his shins, though it was the policeman who shouted at the concrete his shoes seemed to meet.

He'd never had much to do with the police in the Nottinghamshire village where he lived. They existed at a distance, as it were, and Joshua's life hadn't led him closer than that. By accident his actions had been law-abiding. In a strike, however, you could only do as the union advised and your own mates willed, and if it meant pushing up against the coppers then there was nothing else to do but do it.

When suddenly confronted with such ranks of police, he felt, perhaps because numerical superiority was on his side, that they had no right to stand in his way. The atmosphere

41

was so heady that all fear went – that apprehension of danger and readiness to run that he'd often experienced down the pit when a prop was about to go.

Joshua carried a copy of the Bible in the back pocket of his trousers. It was a small black book that went to all places except the pit-face, for he left it with his fags and matches in the locker up top – nothing inflammatory being allowed down below.

Though fifty years of age he had long thought he looked younger than that. He could run faster than might have been expected, lift greater weights than many men of his age who had already been stricken with a hernia, and often work longer hours than were called for.

He played football in the pit team. In fact he did not appear younger than his years, but the confidence he gained by thinking he did gave more life to his face and more authority to his voice. His three sons had married and 'left home', so maybe it was the sudden emptiness of the house that made him feel younger. When grandchildren began to turn up he expected to have the years put back on him ten-fold.

A big man of six-foot-four, he had worked at the pit since he was fourteen, even during the war, so that he'd never been in the army or worn any uniform. Such 'false raiment' was the only thing foreign to his back. All he needed, he said, were sweat-rags on the face when, after going two miles on wide conveyor-belts through darkened neatly hewn tunnels that looked safe but were by no means reliable, and jumping on for a ride with the rest of them when they weren't supposed to, he'd walk awhile and then go on hands and knees to a seam that, being only three or four feet and held apart by a few brace of Doughty props, was 'bloody murder' to work. There were seams so narrow that no machines could be slotted in, though men had to crawl in and rip out the coal nonetheless.

He laboured with the gang, nothing on but Wellingtons up

to the knees when there was water about, lay on his side and swung a pick at the grey-black shine of the fuel, the mellow beam of his head-lamp giving vague illumination through the falling dust.

With half the shift gone they'd knock off, and he'd open his snap-tin to see what Jessie had packed the night before. Whether it was ham or cheese, or a bit of meat and an apple, it made no difference but was turned by a mighty appetite into grub that went into his mouth with any grit picked up on the way. Tea washed it down, and that was the best intake of the lot.

As a child Joshua had never worn shoes, but put on plimsolls to school in summer, and clogs in winter. Later it was either boots or welloes. For best he got a pair of good boots which he polished shinier than any fancy slippers, not too heavy though or hobnailed, but boots of good leather, top and bottom, which held the feet firm and supported the ankles.

'If you aren't well shod,' he said, 'you're nothing. It was all right for the Israelites to go in sandals, but they'd not lived in Nottinghamshire.'

He put on boots when he went to the Welfare Club for a drink in the evening, and wore a high-necked pullover under his jacket to keep out the wind that leapt up the escarpment on which the pit village stood. The houses, built in the twenties, were thought of as new by those who lived in them and saw the black and damp-walled state of other settlements.

Joshua's three-bedroomed house was as comfortable a place as almost thirty years of married life could make it. He'd bought much of his furniture after the war when wages were good, but lately the colliers' 'living standard' had been going downhill fast, and nobody knew it more than he did.

Ever since they'd married he and Jessie had accounted for every penny. Not that they marked each item in a little red cashbook, but nothing was spent that wasn't talked about and remembered – at least till the next wage-packet came in.

They'd never had the pleasure of spending without thought, but at the same time the shared thrift had been enjoyed in that it was one of many factors which had kept them close together.

Being a 'Bible man' Joshua was often the butt of other blokes at the Welfare, and one or two communists who saw his worth thought it a pity he wouldn't join them. Good for an argument, Joshua usually revelled in it, a fact which ought to have told them there was never any hope of converting him to their way of looking at things.

He had his pride, though that didn't keep him from accepting their views. It was just that he liked reading his Bible, obstinately so, and they hadn't such a book, as far as he could see, to put in its place. Those parsons who kept an eye open for him sooner or later found out that it wasn't Christianity which kept his back upright and his face in fettle.

It wasn't that he went to church or chapel even. When Joshua argued about the existence of God with his friends at the club it was more to please himself than to convince them. It was also more to please himself than to please God, for it was the Book he took to, and all the bits in it that highlighted his own existence. They often did, dramatically, and not always in a way he liked.

The New Testament didn't interest him. He'd long since given that up because he couldn't reconcile himself to the 'turning the other cheek' part, being more in tune to the 'eye for an eye' reality of the Old Testament. And as for paying Caesar what was Caesar's, and giving to God what was God's – all right, but what had Caesar ever given him? Nothing. With God it was another matter. Sometimes He gave and sometimes He didn't. In any case, had Caesar ever been down the pit? Not likely – but he didn't doubt that God had been there from time to time. He engendered hope, and gave cause for despair. He gave back life, and He created abysmal misery.

Joshua was popular because he was a good worker who

could be relied on. He wouldn't let anybody down, and his friends felt it, not doubting that he was one of them. He never questioned it, though he'd question everything else. His Bible-mania set him apart, but no more so than his inordinate height. Being separate in several ways merely emphasized his unity with the others, which became even more of a closeness when he was included in it.

The ballot papers came and he voted for the strike. Caesar had to be taken on, even if it meant the destruction of Rome itself.

He dug his garden over the first day, though there wasn't much point with such a frost. In the evening he switched on the television, but could only stand it for an hour because every word spoken and picture shown seemed to be coming straight out of Caesar's tent, never mind his camp. He was filled with bitter loathing when news announcers said that the miners were 'idle' instead of 'on strike'. He switched the set off and picked up his tin of tobacco to roll a cigarette.

'It's going to be a long do,' he said. 'They don't want to know. The truth means nothing to them.'

Since it was wickedness to be still, Jessie knitted pullovers, went at the rate of two a year, and had a drawer full upstairs. She was a tall woman, but thin. 'We'll have to manage.'

He made two cigarettes, and put one back into the tin. 'There's plenty more besides us. The young blokes'll feel it most.'

'They say the country don't need coal any more.'

'They say a lot o' things. Time'll tell.'

'It'll be a long while, though.'

He stood up. 'Nobody denies that. They think they've got us where they want us, forcing us into a strike so's they can finish us off. It's the last thing I wanted.'

'It's early days yet, Josh.'

'It's tragic, though,' he said. 'It's going to be a whole waste of time, and time's the most valuable thing in the world.

45

There's none of us got that much as we can throw it away.'

'Ne' mind. Cheer up, love. We've had worse bouts. I'll put the kettle on. I know you allus get thirsty when you get depressed.'

He smiled at her concern for him. He would have laughed with pleasure, but stopped himself because the reason for his smile was too serious. He thought there was no greater mark of a person's love than when they tried to get you out of a low mood, especially when a woman did it, who had a rough life anyway.

It was unnatural having nothing to do. It made the world empty and took all its meaning away. Coming home from work the trees and buildings were clear because he knew what they were for, but wandering along to the shop at midday without the ache of work in his muscles he felt that even he himself was unreal, right down to the marrow, as if the slightest breath of wind would blow him away.

When a man went to work every day at set hours the aches and pains he might feel if he didn't were crushed out of him. A whole new world opened up when you didn't go to work, and though the first few days had been interesting Joshua didn't want it at all for a permanent set-up. There wasn't much to do, and that was a fact. Few pickets were needed at their own pit, and there were more than enough to sew up all those in the region good and tight.

Squads were sent out to starve the Trent Valley power stations of coal, without which they couldn't work. A new urgency came into the fight, and the union called for volunteers to go south and help the Kent miners, whose coalfield was much smaller than theirs in the Midlands.

Bill Marriot persuaded Joshua: 'Caesar's bloody strong down there, Josh, and our lads in Kent could do with a few reinforcements.'

'When do we start, then?' he asked, the half pint looking no more than a thimble in his hand.

46

'Five in't morning. There'll be six of us in my owd banger. We're going to Greenwich so's we can block the Thames power stations. We'll never get anywhere till we strangle them. Heath'll be playin' his organ by candlelight before we've done.'

Marriot said they wouldn't bother with the motorway because grub was too dear at the service stations. He knew a few good transport caffs on the old North Road.

Joshua's travels and mystery trips had gone no further than Skegness and Bridlington, Blackpool and Matlock. The further south he got the more dispirited he became. Though he'd seen it on televison the landscape looked unreal and soft, and didn't have the pinkish hue of frost or mist that made the Trent Valley so remote and mysterious when the hills on the northern bank merged into the remnants of Sherwood Forest.

To him Notts was a place that stood on its own, too low for the Pennines, too high for the Fens. Neither north nor south, east or west, field or forest, and in some areas neither town nor country, it could hold its own for beauty, obstinacy, and homeliness with any other spot on earth. Joshua realized he only felt that way because he was born there, and he was leaving it now for just as long as it would take them to get enough money to live more comfortably in it.

Even the houses going south were different, less raw and stony and purely useful than the ones where he lived. But the others in the car enjoyed the sights, and laughed when Marriot said they were at last taking the war into the enemy's territory.

Joshua sat in the back hardly able to move, as if their gaiety and confidence was an ungodly force set on kidnapping his true heart and spirit, which should have stayed at home. Pushed into the upholstery so as to give the others more room, he felt the padding and sharp edges of the Bible in his back pocket, and for some reason wished he's left that behind also.

Each two men shared a suitcase for their kit, so that three

47

were roped on to the luggage rack overhead. Room might have been found in one for Joshua's bible, but he didn't trust it to be anywhere except in his pocket.

North of London they needed petrol, and pulled into a filling-station forecourt. All six eased out to get life back into their thighs and ankles, and strolled around in the raw air while Marriot asked for six gallons.

The pump man was the owner as well, and when he saw the notice in their back window saying SUPPORT THE MINERS he turned a different shade of clay-pink: 'I'm not serving you.'

'You what?' Marriot was stunned.

'What does he mean?' Joshua asked. 'Hasn't he got none left?'

'Not a drop,' the man called, slotting his hose back into place. He was a young-looking energetic person in his forties. 'You can try some other place.'

They stood around him by the garage door. 'How far is the next one?' Joshua said, not fully understanding.

'That's your problem. You ought to be driven back to work. I do eighty hours a week and don't get the wages you lot make. By God, I started work at fourteen and I've never stopped going since, night or day. There's no set hours for me.'

'And no set wages, either,' said Marriot. 'You've made your pile all right, I expect. You've never been more than a stone's throw from daylight, either. I'd like to see you do eight hours a week down the pit, ne' mind eighty.'

'If it were my job, I'd do it,' the man said courageously. 'I wouldn't whine and strike about it.'

Because it had taken him longest to understand what was happening Joshua lost his temper sooner than the others when he did catch on. He was not normally a slow man, was known in fact for his picturesque wit and speed of argument, but two hours cramped in the car, and his brooding doubts about coming to this alien part of the realm, had caused him to retreat into himself as a means of self-preservation.

In this mood he did not loom as tall and bulky as he actually was but, seeing an injustice about to be perpetrated on his mates and himself, he held himself fully erect and lifted his fist as he approached the petrol-pump attendant.

'Nay, lad,' he said with false kindliness when he drew back with an offended sneer, 'I'll not touch a hair o' thy Philistine head – even though I am four cubits high.'

The man clearly thought him a maniac on the loose from Rampton, for after this opening Joshua reached into his back pocket and pulled out the flexible fully-fledged Bible and waved it at him (as if it were a lump of coal, Marriot said later) the others looking on, either dumbfounded or cracking with amusement.

'Pharaoh is pursuing us, and we are in dire need of victuals for our chariot. And Moses said unto the people, "Remember this day, in which ye came out of Egypt, out of the house of bondage; for by strength of hand the Lord brought you out from this place." So my advice to you, dear son of a glutton and king of all the idolaters, is to help us to get on our way or we'll verily call the seven plagues to pestificate your inheritance and lay the place as waste as the Desert of Sin.'

Wind drove flecks of rain against Joshua's face so that it looked as if he were weeping with emotion at the godliness of his advice.

'You tell the bastard, Josh,' said Marriot, who saw they might after all be getting somewhere by his harangue. 'And if he wain't listen, throw the bleddy book at him!'

'You won't be served here,' said the proprietor, though plainly worried.

Joshua was more interested in Marriot's advice that he should throw the *bloody* book at him. He reminded him that the Book wasn't to be used like that, nor so wantonly insulted. The Book was God's word and all His works were in it. There

49

was no other Book so blessed by God's advice, and there never would be, and what's more he'd never *throw* it at anyone lest it land in the mud of iniquity or be trodden underfoot by slothful worshippers of the graven image.

He seemed more threatening to Marriot than he had been to the proprietor, who now saw an internecine punch-up as something worse than an assault on himself by this religious bigot who had somehow got entangled in the coal strike. Or it may have been that the proprietor used this swing against Marriot as an opportunity to get out of a dangerous and tricky situation without losing too much face, for he took the hose-nozzle from its bracket, switched the peg on to six gallons, and began sending it into their almost empty tank. 'You can have your petrol,' he said, 'and then go away. I don't want you on my premises.'

Joshua turned from sermonizing Marriot, an ecstatic look on his fully fleshed but pale face: 'Milk and honey,' he said, 'milk and shining honey, lads. Let's pay him and get on to them power stations. He'll be pumping it in by hand next week, and counting his shekels out by candlelight!'

Going through the streets of east London, thumbs-up signs were frequent. At a pub in Hackney a group of bus drivers wouldn't let them pay for their beer.

Marriot took them over the Thames by Tower Bridge, so that Joshua could have a look at it, and see something else he might only have looked at before on television. Joshua was not impressed. Only the river took his gaze, and he thought that maybe he was crossing the Jordan instead of the Thames, and wondered how long it would be before he went back over it.

He felt like removing his Wellingtons before entering the living room. In any case it all opened into one with the kitchen so that you didn't know which was special and which was not, so he narrowed his eyes and decided his boots were good enough for any carpet.

He followed Pam Seymour who, like her husband Jack was a university lecturer, and towered over her as she said with a smile that he was to make himself comfortable while in their house. Marriot had gone scooting off up the road in his car, so there wasn't much else he could do except try.

A dark-haired girl showed him to the spare room with his luggage. He looked around for a moment when she had gone: a wardrobe, a writing table, a narrow bed, and a radiator which almost scalded his hand as he reached out and touched it slyly to see if it was on.

'There's food in the kitchen, at any time,' Pam said, when he came down again as if to see what she would tell him next. 'When you feel hungry just help yourself. Juana our *au pair* girl will show you where things are. We're all behind you in your strike, and *know* you'll win. Jack will drive you to the power station in the morning so that you'll get there well in time for your picketing.'

'That's very kind,' said Joshua, somewhat misled by such consideration. 'I don't want to put him out. I's'll find it on the bus.'

They stood in the kitchen part of the ground floor waiting for the kettle to boil. 'No, we're glad to help. We have a car, so you'll be taken there. We can't do enough for you really. Your fight is our fight.'

It wasn't easy to know what she meant by this, when you looked around to see what they'd got. But he was glad of such comfort and kindness no matter how it came about. He was tired after the journey, felt as if his leg-bones were rotting, and could find nothing to say, almost as if he'd turned into a kid again. He wished Marriot were with him, but they'd put him in another house down the road. Still, the tea was good here. Whoever she was she brewed a black cup of tea, which opened his eyes and made him feel better.

She asked where he came from, and he told her about it,

thinking it impossible she could imagine what it was like. But she'd been there, had become slightly acquainted with such places during sociological research, though she didn't tell him so, being touched by his exaggerating the squalor of it.

He didn't like being given so many questions, but answered them all, till he felt it was his turn, and asked if she had lived 'in this' for long, and whether she'd got any kids?

'Three,' she told him, and he saw from her smile that even though she was turned thirty she still had good teeth. 'They'll be home from school soon. I'm sure they'll be happy to meet you.'

He told her about his own three. 'All married now. But when I look back on it I know me and Jessie enjoyed bringing them up. They were a lot o' trouble, though. But bringing 'em up's the best part of it, any road. After that there in't much left, is there?'

He mused on what it would have been like, being married to such a person as her, this dark, thin-faced, straight-haired, slight-bodied woman who seemed able to deal with the world on her own terms yet could at the same time help others who didn't have that wide and happy grasp of things. A few slots of the picture went through his mind with peculiar clarity, and with perfectly easy realism because it hadn't happened and never would. If it had he would have been another person, though the faint sense of regret that their worlds were so different made him smile – which also brought its feeling of righteousness because it would never do to get too close to the last commandment of the Lord on Sinai. No man's wife would ever be his, nor his any other man's. Having told himself this, the conversation became easier again.

She left him drinking his fourth cup of tea and took a pair of towels up to his bedroom. She saw a Bible on the table and wondered where it had come from. It certainly didn't *belong* in her house, and she looked at it with amusement before realizing it was Joshua's, and flicking the pages from cover to cover.

They'd thought they were getting a member of the Party, and here was a collier carrying a worn, well-thumbed Bible! It was at this moment only that he seemed really strange. Otherwise he was simply a coalminer whom she could never begin to understand. Her father had been the vicar of a potty little church in the west of England, and she hadn't seen much of Bibles since then – thank God!

It was still light when Joshua walked across Blackheath and on to Greenwich Park for a bit of air. The roar of traffic along the road deafened his brain so that he felt isolated and knew he didn't belong where he was standing while waiting to cross. It also seemed he didn't even belong in Nottinghamshire, so that he was disembodied and floating in a strange sort of spiritual emptiness. He tried hard to picture his village or even his own house, but could hardly remember it, though he'd only left that morning.

But the more he walked into the park and over the grass the less this fact troubled him. On the way back he actually felt good to be away, as if he were on some kind of holiday, while knowing that the serious business of what he had come for would begin in the morning.

Pam was getting the children out of her French car, having just fetched them from school. Barney ran up to Joshua and cried: 'Mummy, is this our new miner?'

Joshua felt himself hugged around the legs, so picked him up. '*We've* got a miner now,' Barney sang out. 'Horrid Jasper Clewes at school was boasting that they had *two* miners at their house, but now I can say ya-ya-ya we have one as well!'

'Do leave him alone and come in,' Pam called, though amused and pleased when Joshua walked up the drive with Jerry on his other arm. Matthew, who was ten, thought himself too old for such treatment, so followed enviously behind.

Joshua walked into the local pub that evening. 'I thought I'd find you lot in 'ere.'

'You must have smelled your way,' said Marriot. 'I suppose you couldn't tear yourself from that cushy billet.'

He ordered a pint and went to their table. 'What's *your* digs like, then?'

'Digs?' said Marriot. 'It's real solidarity. As posh as they come. Me and Tom shares a room. Do you snore, Tom?'

'What the bloody'ell does it matter?' said Tom, who did. 'You ain't going to bloody marry me.'

'Not on the wages you get,' said Marriot, 'in any case.'

'Ne' mind,' said Tom. 'I'm out for more!'

Marriot turned to Joshua. 'She's nice, your landlady?'

'Very amiable,' he told them. 'She's got some good kids. I ain't met the husband yet.'

He fell silent, and they were unable to get any more opinions out of him, knowing in fact that he had few enough. Joshua realized it too. It sometimes even embarrassed him, though mostly for the sake of others, for by now he had grown used to his quiescence. His lack of opinion was covered somewhat by his attraction to the Bible, a book which he allowed to hold them for him, often in a highly fashioned picturesque way. He was too shy to attribute such direct and colourful sentiments to his own make-up, in spite of the fact that he might have held them anyway. He was also too firmly latched into life to tell himself whether the ins and outs of it were right or wrong. They just were, and there seemed little else you could do about it. And if there was nothing you could do, what better than to keep silent?

Jack the husband came down for breakfast. Joshua thought he looked younger than his wife, and saw him with a similar slight dark build as he stood up to shake hands while still in his socks. His face was so full of life that Joshua couldn't imagine him able to exert much authority as a university professor, but he had to admit that he didn't know much about that sort of world. He was easy to get on with, and that was everything.

The three children watched Joshua wrapping a copy of the *Guardian* around each ankle and shin. He did it as meticulously as a 1914 soldier applying his puttees before going on parade, but in this case a full tight wrap of a complete newspaper for each leg, over which he pulled his Wellingtons.

He looked at Barney: 'That's if anybody kicks me, should I get into a scrimmage.'

Jack puffed at his pipe, and laughed. 'Who are you expecting kicks from?'

'As if we couldn't guess,' said Pam, who came into the room with a briefcase and a bundle of papers.

'It's not what you expect,' said Joshua. 'It's what you get, though. Or might get, shall we say.'

'They put newspaper there, in case the police kick them,' said Matthew. 'That's what we talk about at school.'

'You sound like a good learner,' Joshua said.

'Can I kick you?' Barney asked.

'As a sort of test, you mean?'

Jack poured himself more tea and frowned. 'That's no way to treat a guest, Barney. We have to bring them up on the right side,' he said, as if someone might doubt his basic principles.

'Come on then,' Joshua said to Barney, 'have a go. If I feel it, I'll give yer a penny.'

Barney took a run, a charge of unconscious buckled-down energy from the other side of the room. His foot struck the boot, and he fell back, toes slightly hurt.

Joshua pulled him close: 'You're a brave lad. I think you deserve a shilling for that. But don't do it every day, will yer?'

Pam said a shilling was too much to give a child, who had twenty pence a week pocket money anyway. Joshua coloured faintly, in case they thought him too mean to give such a fair amount. He put a coin into Barney's hand: 'Now you can tell your smarmy school pals that you've got a collier as well.'

The Kent pickets had organized a Flying Column of thirty cars with six men in each, and ten outriding motorbikes with a pillion passenger – a force of two hundred which both employers and police found hard to handle.

Fighting on 'interior lines', the Flying Column raced from one power station to another as soon as information reached them (generally from their fellow workers inside) that a load of coal was due to be delivered.

News came one morning, after a week at the Thames power station, that 'they' were trying to get coal out of the port gates at Medway. Joshua and the Notts lot got into cars for a great dash along fifty miles of dual carriage-way linking the two rivers. Each man wore the same knee-high Wellingtons that he used down pit, reinforced with a newspaper that turned them to concrete should anyone try to engage in a game of kickshins. This was why, when Joshua found himself in the front rank of the two hundred at Medway dock gates, the policeman shouted with pain on trying to get in a good kick at the collier in front who was pushing a bit too hard for law and order.

The police had been 'thumping the guts' out of the few miners blocking the gate since early morning, but now drew back their lines at the sudden vociferous reinforcement of the Flying Column. Two men had been arrested further along the line, and the inspector who heard the Welsh voice exhort Joshua to 'Get your false teeth into his knackers' swung his track violently into the crush shouting: 'If you come near me, you lousy Welsh Baptist bastard, I'll knock *your* false teeth down your throat.'

It acted on the Welshman like a psychological nail-bomb. But he stayed cool, edged towards the inspector and, apparently out of nowhere, got him around the neck. The crowd opened to let them fight, but another part of it, to which Joshua belonged, got a grip on the Welshman, as friendly as could be had under the circumstances, and pulled him off.

Meanwhile a couple of constables took hold of the police officer and dragged him away.

This was the ugliest moment of the morning, and perhaps the inspector realized his mistake, for he made his way to the van parked by the kerb to consult with other officers who had just arrived. Certainly the colliers knew that if he had tried any more wild talk with the Welshman the riot would have completed itself into what neither police nor union officials would have found easy to stop.

A policeman went across to the lorry trying to get out of the docks and ordered the driver back inside. The gates were then closed, and the miners informed that they would not be opened again until the strike was settled. So they might as well go home.

'Spin me another,' said Marriot, sitting down on the kerb. 'It's a real fight, Josh, every bit o' the way. They can't tell me it's over yet – not by a long fart.'

Joshua rolled a cigarette. 'I expect we'll laugh at it one day. I don't like it, though. There could be a threat to life and limb in it. The Lord's got nowt to do wi' this. It's the Devil, more like.'

'They're devils,' Marriot nodded. 'Give us the Sermon on the Mount, Joshua.'

'I don't read that. I stop at the Prophets.'

'I expect we'll go back to Greenwich,' said Marriot, sounding as if he'd be glad of a rest. 'I need to set my watch anyway.' He pointed across the road: 'Just bloody look at that, will yer' – where a police canteen van was providing tea, and a few miners were standing around drinking from paper cups the police must have given them. 'What a bloody lot of scroungers. They'd scrounge owt, the boggers. They'd scrounge milk out of a virgin's tit, they would.'

'Don't go on about it,' Joshua said, blinking. 'I suppose the coppers have got soft hearts as well, some of 'em. They're only like us, if you tek that false raiment off their backs.'

Marriot's eyes were sharp for other things, and beamed on a gate further along the road which the majority of pickets had somehow neglected. A huge lorry with high wooden sides, and laden with small pieces of coal, steered out and made off along the road towards the motorway as fast as it was possible to accelerate.

'Come on,' Marriot cried, leaping up.

They ran to the nearest car. A driver was already at the wheel, but so many others were trying to get in that it was almost a minute before it drew away with a clattering roar.

Joshua was by the driver, peering through traffic for a glimpse of the lorry, which seemed to have totally avoided them. 'There ain't much we can do even if we catch it up,' Marriot said from the back seat. 'They pulled a bloody fast one on us all right, the sly gets. Some blokes 'ud sell their souls for a barrel of beer and a kipper.'

'Maybe only a cup o' tea,' said Joshua, who felt himself sweating from sudden heat in the car. His heart beat nervously from the chase. 'Just keep looking.'

It was impossible for him to be comfortable with the Bible so sharp at his back pocket, but now he was almost trying to stand with the effort of looking along the road ahead.

'He's turned off somewhere,' Marriot suggested.

'That's more than he dare do,' said Joshua. 'We'd corner him then like a rat. He'll keep straight on, yo' see.'

'Not that he'll find it easy to drive his load into any power station, man,' the Welsh driver said, overtaking a car and a bus. 'The boys are waiting for the likes of him.'

'They might have another secret gate for him to get into,' said Joshua. 'We must nab him on the way there.' But nobody knew how.

The lorry was labouring up a slip road leading to the motorway. They saw it. The car was faster and more agile, and was soon behind, under the towering rear wall of it.

'Only wish he don't start rolling back,' said the driver. 'Be

58

the end of my promising career' – and his words made them laugh, a near hysterical chorus which sharply ceased when they began wondering what to do.

It was drizzling, and he flicked the wipers on to get rid of grit and oil-slick coming at them from the big wheels. 'We're so close on his tail,' said Marriot, 'that he don't know we're there.'

The driver of their car changed to bottom gear. 'He's crawling like a worm. Packed everything on, the greedy swine.'

'He'll get a fat bonus,' said Marriot. 'Right up his arse, I hope. The thing is, though: What do we do now?'

'How fast is he going?' Joshua asked

'Same as us,' said the Kentish Welshman. 'About ten, I would say.'

Joshua opened the door. 'Leave it to me.'

'You'll kill your bloody self,' Marriot shouted.

'I'll be all right. Can you keep a bit back from the lorry, Taffy? As long as the Lord stays with me. I don't want my guts crushing in. Just a bit behind. Then watch.'

Taffy nodded, his face plainly worried when Joshua got out of the car and closed the door quietly as if the lorry-driver in front might hear it. He ran alongside in great strides, like a giraffe.

His breath grated as he worked, hoping the slope was long enough to keep the lorry going slow while he did what was in his mind. The steel pin along the bottom of the wooden back wall was stiff as he tried to loosen it.

It was no use tugging at the bar, for it was solidly in position, so he first lifted the end up and down to try and ease it. His Wellingtons were a liability, as if they were full of wet sand. Black grit from the lorry wheels sprayed out and over, almost blinding him, so that he was continually wiping it away, working with a permanent squint.

He saw a vision of the Lord, fire on Mount Pisgah, and knew

the strength of the walls of Jericho. His hands slipped on the cold metal, but it became easier, and with one hard pull in which all his muscle and breath was used, he began to draw it away.

Then it stuck for what seemed the rest of his life, and he saw the Angel of Death, and ten thousand Egyptian chariots ready to fall and sweep him into the blood-red sea of blackness.

It seemed as if he'd taken on more than he could handle, and he felt for a moment at the Bible banging loose in his trousers behind. Then he ran to catch up with the lorry of the Pharisees, and work harder than he'd ever worked in his life.

The bar was a quarter of the way across and he planned his leap clear should the avalanche of coal come down from the sky, aimed as it would be straight at his head and vulnerable body which seemed small enough to him now. He thought of the car trailing a few yards from his heels, but daren't look at it, knowing beyond doubt that they'd seen his renewed hope and further progress.

It was raining more heavily, but in a way he welcomed it because the icy sloosh cooled and comforted him, eating up the hot sweat from his face as he ran. The bar was half-way across, and at three quarters over he could leap clear because it would come the rest of the way by itself. A few lumps of coal were already banging on to his Wellingtons.

With the finest show of timing, born of knowing when the creak of the Doughty prop was at the breaking point and one had to scramble clear, he left the bar to do its own work, for it was down at the road and striking sparks from it. Half a hundredweight of best power-station coal had already fallen. He glanced over his shoulder, a look which Marriot said later was full of rabbit-panic.

The car was close by, yet it was out of his grasp, a mile away, and impossible to reach. As the coal fell he had a feeling of death, of dropping also into an emptiness so wide and complete that his consciousness was for a moment obliterated. Sky, road, and coal no longer existed. It was like going to sleep on the job: when you came out of it a hundred years might have passed, but in reality it was only a second. Something went into his mind during that short vacuum of time, and he didn't know what it was, only that in all his years down the pit he'd never been so close to it before.

He had pins and needles in front of the eyes, an aching clarity that made him want to shut out the sharp detail of the lorry-back. Then he saw Marriot looking from the car and beckoning madly. He nipped to the side and pulled at the half-open door as it drew level.

Nobody spoke as he got into his seat. Hearts and eyes were fixed on the menacing wall of the lorry shedding its coal, now breaking on them. The driver, with a soft and melodious curse (followed by a prayer for their safety) turned the wheel and eased on to the outer lane to avoid the avalanche.

They followed in this position till the whole of several tons had fallen, and paved the road behind for a good mile. The driver inside the lorry, still perhaps full of his triumph at out-witting the colliers, and thinking of the promised bonus, drove without realizing the unexpected twist that had befallen him.

They got on to the motorway, and put on speed to seventy miles an hour. Ten miles must have passed before the driver reached over to Joshua, his hand outstretched: 'Shake it, there's a good man. I've never seen anything like it.'

Marriot was laughing hysterically in the back, already think-ing of telling it that night to the others in the pub. He knew he would have a monopoly of the tale, because Joshua wouldn't say much about it.

Joshua took the Welshman's hand, and held it as if they were both children who needed the solid reassurance of love that only children can give each other. Then he let go and felt behind him. The angular sharpness had gone from his back pocket. He'd no longer got his Bible – the old, only, long-loved book of life and leisure bought as a youth from a stall in

61

Worksop market place. It must have jumped out during his frantic work, and been buried under thousands of black coal-lumps. He felt like a mountain crumbling into sleep.

The pay terms were announced, and accepted. They had got what they wanted. The government had given in. With so many troops in Northern Ireland it could not afford to fight the miners as well.

Joshua was neither glad nor disappointed. They could beat Caesar any time. But he wanted to get back, back to where he came from so that he could feel real again. He felt a need to get himself back into the pit and rip out that coal from under the earth.

He sat in the kitchen, having packed two carrier bags with his things. Pam came in to give him a meal before the journey north. She would be sorry to see him go. It was as if he had lived in the house for a long time. He belonged to it almost.

'Are they your things, Josh?'

'That's 'em.'

'Do you have your Bible?'

He coloured slightly. She wondered why he was embarrassed at her mentioning it, when he hadn't been before. He didn't know she knew he'd lost it, because he'd mentioned it to no one. 'It got misplaced,' he said, seeing no reason for secrets.

'I hear you lost it in a scrimmage,' she said.

He laughed, and she was surprised to see an elderly man so shy. It made him look young: 'I'll get another sort of Bible, I expect. I'm never too old to learn.'

'It's true,' she said.

He nodded. 'I suppose it would have been better to have learned things a bit younger, though. We can get 'em on the run any time o' day or night. It's been a bit of an education, you might say.'

His carrier-bags weren't packed neatly enough, so he bent down to rearrange the things inside. Pam went out, and came back with a suitcase: 'Put your things in this.'

'It's done,' he told her.

'I hope you'll come and see us when you're in London. We'll never forget you. Especially the children. Barney cried last night when I told him you had to go.'

She took a platter of chops from the oven. It was the *au pair*'s day off. 'Jack and I are so glad about it all.'

'We had a lot of help,' he said, beginning to eat.

She put his things in the suitcase, determined that he should take it, having talked it over with her husband the night before. 'You'll need it when you come down again – or go anywhere else on your travels.'

'There's no need,' he said, but seeing he was embarrassing her by refusing he added: 'It's very good of you.'

He was glad she repacked his things out in the hall because he'd be able to eat without being looked at. Marriot would be round with the car in half an hour. The only woman he could bear to have looking at him while he was eating was Jessie. It was marvellous how people stuck together during a strike. He didn't feel young any more. There was more to life than that. He'd not forget the different men from coalmines around the country he'd met. It certainly was one land when you thought of it like that. All he'd known was the black guts he sweated in among the dust and shale. Now he knew a bit more about the top of it.

When he thought of the coal he'd spilled over the road he couldn't believe he was still alive, though it seemed a terrible waste. There was some malice when he brought back the memory and laughed over it. With so many endings in life it was good to have a happy one for a change.

But all he wanted to do was rip more coal out of the earth, now that Caesar had been put in his place – for a while.

BEFORE SNOW COMES

The lights below glowed red like lines of strawberries. Snow had been forecast, and when it fell he thought they would be buried. The smell of frost and smoke had softened, and he could taste snow on his lips even before the first flake drifted down on to his hair.

The only thing was to drink, drink, drink, and try not to forget. With glass after glass her face came back with much greater clarity than when he was sober. In full ordinary everyday light she stayed dim and far away, out of sight and all possibility of mind. But in memory she never stood so close that he could touch her.

He recognized the garden because of the rosebush growing in it. The palings leaned as if they would never get up again. They had not been thumped by a good-natured drunk, for then they could have been willingly straightened, but sagged as if someone had deliberately kicked them in passing because he was fed up with life when he had no need to be. They should be totally uprooted and thrown away for bonfire night. Then I'd get some of those new-smelling planks and laths from the woodyard and put good fences around that rosebush. He would get clean steel nails and set out those laths and offshoot wasted planks from the trunks of great trees that he got cheap because one of his mates worked there, and brush off the sawdust lovingly from each one, feeling it collect like the wooden gold-dust of life in the palm of his hands and sift between the broad flesh of his lower fingers. That half-sunk sagging fence wanted a good dose of the boot, to be followed of course by a bit of loving skill for her sake.

He had it because he was divorced. His spirit was turned upside down, the sand in his brain rifting through as in the old days to body and heart, an eggtimer letting its intoxication into the crevice of every vein and vesicle, bone and sinew. He worked and worked, walked from one step to another between elevation and misery. At work they thought him a happy and reliable mate, but every second night he forgot to wind up his watch and had to call on a neighbour to check the time in order to say hello in the morning, otherwise he'd be late getting up for work (or might never get up at all) and that would never do.

He had four brothers and two sisters, all of them married, and all divorced, except one who was killed in a car crash. It wasn't that his family was unlucky or maladjusted, simply that they were normal and wholesome, just conforming like the rest of the world and following in the family tradition with such pertinacity that at the worst of times it made him laugh, and at the best it sent him out in carpet slippers on Sunday morning to buy a newspaper and read what was happening to other families. What else could you do and think, if the razor-blade of fate isn't to cut you down and spare you even more sufferings? Sometimes he thought he'd buy a Bible and make prayer-wheels to send zipping into outer space, which seemed the only possible alternative to drinking himself to death, which he couldn't afford to do. But the world keeps going round, and it was no use asking what had happened to all the good times. The ocean was too deep and wide to escape from the island on which he found himself.

She kept her roses well, and he remarked on them when passing the backyard where her fence was ready to lie down and never get up again, though it wasn't the worst of them in that terrace by any means. She leaned on the gate smoking a cigarette, a young woman with dark short curly hair, sallow and full in the face below it. Her eyes, a sharp light-blue, gave her expression a state of being lit up and luminous, aware of everything inside her but not of the world. Why she was standing there he didn't know, because there was nothing to look at but a brick wall two yards away. He stopped, nothing else in his mind except: 'I like those roses. I could smell 'em as I went by.'

'They aren't exactly Wheatcroft specials,' she said, not smiling.

'Where'd you get 'em?'

'My brother lives in Hertfordshire, and he gen me a few cuttings from his garden. Only one took, but look how it blossomed!'

'It has, an' all,' he said. Neither of them could think of anything else to say.

'Good-bye, missis.'

'Good-bye, then.'

He didn't see her for a long time, but thought about her. He worked at a cabinet-making factory as a joiner, making doors one week and window frames the next, lines of window frames and rows of doors. The bandsaws screamed all day from the next department like the greatest banshee thousand-ton atomic bomb rearing for the spot-middle of the earth which seemed to be his brain. Planing machines went like four tank engines that set him looking at the stone wall as if to see it keel towards him for the final flattening, and then the milling machines buzzing around like scout cars search for the answers to all questions . . . It was like the Normandy battlefield all over again when he was eighteen, but without death flickering about. Not that noise bothered him, but he often complained to himself of minor irritations, and left the disasters to do their worst. It was like pinching himself to make sure he was alive.

He gave her names, but none seemed to fit. Her face was clear, but he couldn't remember what clothes she had been wearing. It was just after midday and he wrenched his memory around like wet plywood to try and remember if the smell of any cooking dinner had been drifting from her kitchen door, whether she'd been leaning there waiting for her husband to come up the street from the factory. He expected that she had, though it didn't seem important.

After heavy spring rain the Trent flowed fast at Gunthorpe,

as if somebody was feeding it along the narrows with an invisible elbow and tipping it towards the weir that was almost levelled out. But after rain there was sunshine and he cycled up the hill. At Kneeton hamlet he stood at the top of the hill with his bike, looking down through the gloomy bracken, along the descending hedge-tunnel towards the ferry and over the opposite flat bank. But for a better view he turned and leaned his bike against a wall, and went into Kneeton churchyard. The river was as grey as battleship paint, none of the small white clouds of the sky visible in it. They were reflected rather on the glistening fields beyond, and the dry red-roofed houses of various farms and villages.

He walked over the soddened grass, around the small cemetery. The gravestone of Sarah Ann Gash had split in the middle and fallen. She was born on September 1st but it didn't say what year because the split of the slate had gone right through it. Where was Sarah now? he wondered, Sarah who no longer walked around these high woods and looked now and again across the Trent for signs of storm and sunshine.

He'd left his room early, hoping to get in the full brightness of Sunday before the piss of heaven belted down again. He looked across the valley as he'd done dozens of times and brooded on it as he always did, a valley fair and shallow as himself. He told himself it was different now, without being sharp enough at the moment to know why. Locked in his Nottinghamshire room he thought about the past, but seeing this blue sky and so much open land, he wondered about the future, though in such a way that he would allow no useful answer to come out of his musing. He doubted that an answer could come under any conditions, though however unsatisfied he did not want to return to his room and brood without the benefit of such good and placid scenery.

He was a man of forty who considered that nothing had happened in life so far – apart from the death of his parents, and the loss of his wife and child by a divorce which she had

70

wanted, and been willingly given. Just as he believed that a clerk did not work because you could not see his calloused hands and blackheads dotting his face, so he believed that he hadn't suffered because he wasn't physically scarred, crippled, or blind. It seemed that a sense of realism regarding the world and what it could do to you, and you to it, hadn't yet given him the opportunity of being fully born to its wrath, and whenever he felt something near to peace – gazing for too long over the snaky Trent and slowly rising fields on the far side – his face looked more puzzled than pleased. The wind blew against his jersey shirt, and he felt it to the flesh. Anything he felt, he noticed, and this if nothing else brought a smile to his face.

The lane descending to the river went between high hedges with sharp buds scattered over them like green snow, bent slightly on its route to the narrow band of meadow bordering the river-bank. A smell of wet cloud and fields came from the bushes. He wanted to reach the river, but not to plough in his bike and boots through the mud when a paved lane behind would get him there in a little more time but far less trouble.

Four great engines were detonated against the sky, and over the trees to his right a huge plane slid off an aerodrome runway and carried its grey belly far off across the opposite flat fields, suddenly climbing and merging completely with the sky like a bird. Something in him waited for a blue-white flash along the body, a silent unobtrusive packed explosion that would make it vanish for ever from both world and sky, as if it had no right up there where only birds of flesh and feathers could travel. But when it went on its flight he was happy and relieved that nothing happened to it. There is something greater than love, he thought. Far greater. I feel it, something that makes love seem primitive. I can't say what it is, but I know that it exists, though one can only get to it through love.

71

He cycled over the long tarmac bridge, considered stopping on the pavement to look at the river's floodspeed over the parapet, but knew it finally could only interest a child, so turned across the line of traffic and down the lane towards field and gravel-stones sloping between the inn and the water's edge. The nearby weir was almost level yet still let out a thunderous roar of water from its depths, and in various side-pools of the river men sat fishing, oblivious to it. He lay his bike down, and set off for a walk.

A woman and two children were picnicking beyond the first clump of bushes, and not having a very good time of it. A khaki groundsheet had been fixed on two sticks as a shield against the irritating windbite gusting across the river to scatter sandwich papers and salt. They crouched under it, and he heard the grit of discontented voices. It was difficult to light a cigarette in such a cunning wind, except by opening his jacket and holding it as a buffer. So as not to intrude upon their private feast he walked behind them, but when he was closest he knew he had seen the woman before, leaning against the backyard gate of a house in Radford. A boy of seven felt under a blanket and pulled out a transistor radio the size of a two-ounce tobacco tin, and switched on a thin screech of music. Ducks flew over from the woods, and when their beaks moved during a low swerve towards the fishermen behind, he heard no sound because of the radio.

The mother switched it off: 'You can play it after you've had something to eat' – and gave him and his sister a hardboiled egg. He heard the soft crack of shell on a stone, and remembered that he had eaten no breakfast. Her thick plum-coloured coat was open to show a pale-green sweater. His stare drew her head around, and he was astounded now that he had a full view of her face, to see how much it had altered, or how much his memory had embellished it with features it had probably never possessed. The sallowness lay on thinner and smaller bones, and she was darker under her eyes. But she drew him with the

72

same force, like a girl he'd been in love with as an adolescent and just by accident met again, suddenly bringing back to him youth and naïvety and the unforgettable depth and freshness of first love that he knew could never come twice in anybody's lifetime. It struck him that whenever he thought of something that happened a few years ago it always felt as if he were recapturing adolescence.

He stood back, but said when she looked hard at him: 'I was passing, and recognized your face. You live down Radford, don't you?'

'Who's that, mam?'

'Shurrup and get your picnic.' She was puzzled, and not pleased at this plain intrusion.

'I remember your rosebush,' he said with a smile. 'How's it getting on?'

'Not very well. I didn't know you knew me.'

'I passed your gate, and yours was the only back garden with roses in it.'

She gave each child a radish, and the girl who got the biggest held it like a doll, then grasped the green sprouts and chewed it while thoughtfully looking at the river. 'What's your name?'

'Jean,' she said, 'if you like.'

He smiled. 'That's a funny way of putting it.'

'Jean then, whether you like it or not.'

'We talked about your roses. Don't you remember?'

She pulled her coat to. 'Wipe your nose, Paul. Don't let it go all over your food. A lot's happened since.' She was not eating, handled all food respectfully and passed it to her children. A gang of boys went by, waving sticks and swinging tadpole jars at the end of string.

'That's lucky,' he said, 'no matter how bad it is.'

'I don't care, one way or the other.' Yet her face had relaxed almost into a smile in the few words bartered since he'd stopped.

'That's no way, either,' he said. 'You know what they say about Don't Care?' The boy and girl looked up at him, with more interest than their mother. The girl smiled, waiting.

'It goes like this, I think:

> 'Don't Care had golden hair
> Don't Care was green at the face
> Don't Care was tall and lame
> Don't Care wore a shirt of lace
> Don't Care took the Devil's name
> Don't Care was hung:
> Don't Care fell down through the air
> Into a pit of dung!'

He felt foolish at such recitation, yet less so when he saw that all three were amused.

'Where did you learn that?'

He winked. 'Read it in a book.'

'What sort of book?' asked the boy.

'Any book. No, I tell a lie. I remember my father saying it to me as a boy.'

'A rum thing to tell a child,' she said. Wet blue clouds were coming eastwards over the summit of the woods, cold grey at the edges, but a line of sun still cut the mother from her children, moving and warming them in turn.

'I hope it doesn't think to rain,' she said.

'So do I. I biked up from Nottingham, and now I'm off for a walk. What happened to you in the last two years, then?' He saw she wouldn't want to talk about it, but asked just the same, because it was up to her to decide, not him.

'It's a long story,' she said, snubbing him by the silence that followed.

It must be a bloody bad one, he thought, from the way she looks: 'I'll tell you one thing, though: no stories have an ending. They never end. So maybe it won't turn out to be as

74

bad as you think. Take me, for instance. I'm only really happy when I'm working.'

His way of speaking had aroused her interest, as if she was unaccustomed to hearing people speak at all. She asked if he lived alone.

'I do,' he said.

'Me too; but I've got two kids. You keep yourself looking well and clean for a man who lives alone!'

He laughed: 'It's not too difficult.'

'Some men find it so.'

'I'll be going for a stroll then.'

'What's your name, anyway?'

'Mark,' he told her. 'Maybe I'll pass your house again for another look at your roses. I've never seen such fine ones in Radford.'

He climbed a gate and made his way through wet nettles that came up to his knees and brushed his trousers above the tops of his leather boots. Across the path striated puddles barred his way, an edge of the yellow round sun reflected in them. The sky was blue and heavy, patched, rimmed, and streaked with thinning grey cloud. Whenever faced with a long walk he began to feel self-indulgent, wished he hadn't set out, and speculated on his point of no return. The fields stretched into the distance, reluctant to slope up through mist into the hills beyond Southwell. He stood by the edge of a copse that barred his way, black trunks and evergreen tops forming an impenetrable heart in his path. There was a paralysis in his legs that would not allow him to find the free flow around it so as to continue his roaming. What was the point in going on if you could not get easily to the heart? Two pigeons flew out of the field and buried themselves in it without difficulty. It looked even more of a job to get into that than one's own soul, a million times harder, in fact.

It started to rain. The soul was a moth fluttering in smoke, down on the concrete floor of his personality, sometimes touching it with the tips of its wings, flying above it, but always conscious that it was there in the smoke and darkness, and that it could never get through to the richer fields below, where connection with the universe and the clue to the real meaning of life lay. He could not burst that concrete as others presumably had, blast a way through to his soul with the dynamite of hardship and suffering. It was a mystery to him how it was done. Where does one begin? What is the secret or quality of disposition towards nature that one must have in one's marrow? Two pigeons, back out of the copse, were flying through the rain towards the river, and without thinking he headed back in that direction himself. Jean and her children had packed up and gone — which didn't surprise him because the thin consistent rain already reached through to his skin. He rubbed the beads of water from his bicycle handlebars and rode with head down along the main road back towards Nottingham.

The rose bushes had indeed withered: some organic malevolence had bitten them at the root and travelled up to every point of life. The blight had crippled it, in spite of all hope and intermittent care between bitter and useless quarrels with her husband. His departure had been the talk of the yard, but everyone had known right from the beginning that their marriage had been broken-backed and would dissolve one day. So did Jean know, now that it was all over. Even the children had stopped asking for him after a few weeks, knowing that to go on doing so would make her unendurably irritable for hours.

She tried to revive them, bought various compost powders from the ironmonger's and dug up the rock-cake soil around each one, but they seemed unwilling to risk flowering in the closed-off urban air. Their thorns stayed rusty in summer, shining under the blue complacent sky.

While cooking the children's breakfast she remembered the man who had talked to them on their last excursion to Gunthorpe. If only it had been as fine a day as this, she thought, glancing out of the window at a clean warm sky, I'd have felt more like chatting him back instead of driving him away with megrims and miseries. She could find excuses for it, but no reason, though the memory by no means depressed her as she stirred porridge and put sausages under the grill. They had a meal at school, and got their own tea till she came in at six. As for men, she did not care if she never had another one near her for the rest of her life. She'd had two bellyfuls from Ken, and got no joy out of either. Any of that, and she could manage it herself, as most self-respecting women had to do.

Janice came down, dressed already, but Paul still had his pyjama-bottoms on and his clothes bundled up like a bomb under his arm. She snapped and tugged him into a dressed creature in two minutes, and Janice was pouring cold milk into his porridge when she went out of the back door to catch the bus for work.

Mark cycled over in his dinner hour, but she wasn't in. He didn't like being seen in his overalls, but was able to look towards her back door while smoking a cigarette, careful not to lean on the sagging fence which looked as if it would stay up for ever it was so rotten. The neighbours assumed he was her boy-friend, and couldn't understand that someone who must have crept into her house now and again when it was dark – though no one had actually seen him – should be so gormless as to come here in the middle of the day merely to stand and look at the scullery window.

I ought to mend that fence, he told himself. A few good posts and a line of deep holes filled with concrete, and I'd ram in the supports to last till the slum clearance brigade comes round. Wouldn't take me a day.

He'd had the disease most of his life of asking questions

before the time was ripe – if it ever was – and so destroying what pleasure he might be destined to feel if he did the impossible and kept his mind closed. But at half past eight that evening (while it was still light: The neighbours thought he had a cheek) he knocked at the back door with a definite proposition in mind.

A large white towel was swathed around her sopping head, just up from its final rinse at the scullery tap. The two top buttons of her blouse were open, and he turned red at the face. 'I was passing, so I thought I'd say hello.'

'Oh!' she said, the green-eyed twilight blank and clear at the back of his head. 'It's you! I thought it was going to be Flo Holland. What do you want?' The offputting brutality of this abrupt question was lessened by assumption in her tone that he had a right to come there and want something, and that for some reason she by no means considered him a total stranger. Her face seemed less pale, a little more healthy with the dark hair invisible, lines slightly hard like a woman's in a bathing cap and devoid of make-up or lipstick. Through the main window he saw the white electric flash of the telly reflection. 'I've just washed my hair,' she said. 'It saves a few bob to do it at the sink. You can come in for a cup of tea in a minute.'

She closed the door, and he was sure she'd forget him, accidentally-on-purpose, as it were. He stood by the fence smoking, only this time on her side of the gate, and it was amazing how strong that gate looked in comparison to the rotten decrepit lines of paling on either side.

When he was about to walk away the door pulled open. The scarf that bundled the drying hair gave her a gipsy look, darkened her eyes and narrowed the face. 'Come on,' she said, 'I've got the kettle on.' Sometimes when cycling he would go for miles deep in thought, and suddenly realize he could not remember passing any of the familiar landmarks on the road behind. So now, filled with happiness instead of thought, he could not recollect details of getting to the table and facing

78

her from his abstracted melancholy stance by the gate.

'What made me call,' he said, 'was the sight of that fence.'

'I thought it was me,' she said.

'Don't get sarky. I'm a chippie and can fix it for you.'

'How much do you want for it?' she asked.

'I'll do it for fun.'

She held a slice of bread at the fire with a long fork. 'I wouldn't bother. It's been like that for so long. Anyway, if we have a bad winter like the last one I'll use it for firewood to save me or the kids queuing at the coke-yard.'

'The toast's burning,' he said. She buttered it, and poured a mug of tea. 'I don't eat till the kids are upstairs. I get indigestion at their antics. When Paul broke a cup tonight I screamed as if somebody had thrown a knife at me. Frightened the poor little bogger out of his wits.'

'No use getting nervous,' he laughed.

'It's no use telling me that. I was born like it.'

'Who wasn't? Sometimes it goes.'

'In middle age,' she said, 'I'm waiting.'

'There's a long time yet,' he said.

She leaned over for a light. 'Ever go to the pubs?'

'Not as a rule. Do you?'

'Not really. It'd get me out a bit if I did, I suppose.'

'Where do you go for your holidays?' he said.

'You met me on them.'

'Up Gunthorpe?'

'I take the kids now and again. Last year it was Matlock for the day, boating on the Derwent and then into the caves. They enjoyed it, I'm glad to say. We have better times since Ken left, though there's a bit less money to throw around.'

'I expect he'll be back,' he said, as if very happy at the idea.

'When the kids asked me where he'd gone – they didn't like him all that much, but they missed him at first – I said he was off to work in London for a while. But they know he won't come back. I was down town a few weeks ago with Janice, and we was just crossing the road in Slab Square when a bus stopped at the traffic lights, and out of the window I heard this voice shout: 'How are you, Jean, my duck?' and when I looked it was him sitting there as large as life with another bloody woman! Janice asked me who it was so I said it was nothing to do with us, and pulled her round when she tried to look. No, he'll never come back to me. Not that it would do him much good if he tried. More tea?'

'Please. I'll do that fence on Saturday. I often go to work then, but I can leave off overtime for once.'

Neighbours stopped and looked into the small of his back as they passed along the yard, or from the end of it turned to see what he was on with. Clouds were low, and the heavy oppressive warmth of summer weighed over the kitchens and lines of lavatories. Once started on a job he didn't want to stop till it was over and done with. It was a change from making the eternal doors and windows at the factory. He uprooted the rotten palings and prised out rusty nails so that he could lay each piece of redundant wood under the front window for next winter's kindling. The holes were plotted with a ruler, marked by temporary sticks while he mixed the concrete. He'd pushed the new palings up on two journeys by bike the evening before, and she grumbled but gave in when he insisted on them staying overnight in the kitchen. Out in the garden, someone would be bound to pinch them, as he had done.

Janice and Paul watched, chewing caramels he'd treated them to. 'You're making a good job of it,' Jean said, bringing a mug of tea.

'I might as well, while I'm at it.'

'I'm off shopping. I shan't be long' – as if he should be embarrassed left all alone in a strange yard.

He straightened and took the tea. The first three posts were in, packed upright by bricks. 'If you're going out to do a week's shop you might need some money. Take this' – holding a few pounds.

'No,' she said, with a finality that he could neither change nor broach, 'it's all right.'

He crushed the notes back in his hand, fingers kneading till the knuckles went white, hoping they would disappear and prove he hadn't been so stupid as to offer it.

'I'm not being fussy,' she smiled, 'but I just don't need it. You're doing enough as it is.'

'It's good tea,' he said, 'and I was ready for it. I thought I'd help out, that's all.' He took off his cap and rubbed the sweat back into his hair. 'Do you play draughts?'

Arms were folded under her breasts, drawing in her blouse. 'Not for years, but I can.'

'I'll give you a game tonight.'

'All right then. I'll bring some fags back.'

He couldn't refuse them, as she had rebuffed him over the money; in fact such fine tenderness on her part sent as much pleasure through him as if they had indulged in a secret and unexpected kiss.

When the fence was finally up, and the kids packed off to bed, they sat down to a peaceful supper of sliced meat and farmhouse bread, coffee and pickles, cobs and jam. 'You've worked hard,' she said, 'and I'm glad of what you've done.'

'I've worked hard,' he said, his mouth full. 'Hard or soft, it's all the same. It'll stand up a long while. I'll guarantee that.'

They went through three games of draughts, and he beat her every time, though the last one wasn't so easy. 'I don't think we'll play any more,' he laughed, standing to put on his jacket. He felt in a pocket for his clips. 'Ever thought of taking a lodger?' he said, looking close at her.

She had, but wouldn't say so. It was too soon. He came close to kiss her, but she pushed him gently away and went with him to the door. She liked him, because he seemed to think about everything and took nothing for granted. What's more, he was kind and helpful, and such a man was rare. The sky was clear, but stars weren't often in it. Only telly aerials and chimneys were between you and the sky, and they helped to keep you warm.

'I'll think about it,' she said, touching his arm.

He seemed dejected, being at the end of the best day he'd spent in years, as he walked up the yard and out by his new-made fence.

The gate clicked, so she shut the door and went back to clear the table.

He didn't come for a month, but every day she expected him. She saw her husband several times in various parts of the city, but never once did she bump into Mark. Why doesn't he come? she wondered. He builds a brand-new marvellous fence, and then thinks he can just go off like any cock-a-doodle dandy and say no more about it. I suppose he can, she thought, sitting alone one night. He must have been offended when I wouldn't take money towards my shopping, but that's just like a man, to get haughty when they can't make a kept woman out of you in the first five minutes. They either do nothing, or want to do everything too quickly.

But he was close to her, so near, so close that sometimes she could see him clearly, though if she tried to touch him he vanished. She waited for him, but it seemed he'd gone for ever, either because he was scared of her and two children, or because he'd been discouraged by her coldness. She considered herself more hot-blooded than he knew, and as proof thought of the many times she had not been able to tolerate the know-ledge of her husband going to bed with other women, until all vestige of love between them had been destroyed. Even Ken lost his jauntiness, and often his desire for whoever he was running after at the time. Their continual battles were fought with such unplanned unconscious spite that a note of fate and heroism crept into them both, bent as they then became on the complete destruction of each other's emotional base. Neither won, and neither lost – unless Ken could be said to have done so because he was the one who had walked out. She used to think during such fighting that the longer two people lived together the less possible did it become for them to do so. When she didn't speak to him for three days, at least not to say anything civilised, the atmosphere seemed to be damaging her actual brain cells, as if she would never again be able to see anything clearly without the most desperate effort. And when she did nothing else except speak to him for three days it was just as much of a torment, and the damage seemed to be even worse, because neither had a civil word left to say to each other.

But these memories vanished as soon as she thought of Mark, and she felt almost happy again. Then he came back.

He felt the soft warmth of midsummer, and an agreeable wind whose noiselessness was drowned by a gentle continuous brush of incoming water. For the first time in his life he was at peace not only with the world but also with those who lived in it. The clash of the children's spades into the stones sounded somewhere beyond his closed eyes. It was impossible to brood on the misery that had brought such good fortune. The sea excluded all unnecessary reflection. Its rhythms cut him off from any past machinery that may have had control over him. The place he lay on was a bridgehead on the land, and the stones pressing under his body were all that he owned. He reached out and met Jean's thigh, lifted higher until he could take her hand and press it tenderly. You went near the sea so that it could claim you, though it never did, dared it to send up an arm to try and pluck you off the precipitous shelf of life and happiness you had just by a miracle found, and drag you back to the death of its depths where you had come from. It couldn't. Both of them were firm in that. You were dreamy, and in any case had chosen a calm summer's day to lie there when there could be no danger whatsoever.

Jean sat up to spread their lunch, and he heard the children

83

throw down spades and pull themselves over without standing up. 'Mark,' she said, 'I can't get the tops of these flasks off.'

'Knock 'em with a stone. That'll loosen 'em.'

She threw a pebble which struck his shoe. 'If you don't move I'll kiss you, lazy good-for-nothing.'

'Kiss me.'

She bent over, the sea on her lips, hair cutting out light when he opened his eyes. 'You weren't so lazy in bed last night.'

'The mattress was hard.' He jumped up yelling from a sharp nudge in the ribs, then got on his knees to twist the caps off. He couldn't screw his eyes down to the very stones and earth they sat on, but stared vacantly while exerting his strength, towards the far-off grey breakwater that divided a pale blue sea and a pale blue sky, its nearer arm coming out from grey shingle and off-white cliffs. They had come for a fortnight on his hundred pounds saved, taken two rooms half an hour inland on the uppers of the town, but with a wide view over the sea.

At night when the kids were sleeping they went to the front, along it and back, the sky still on fire and the sea blood-black and flat, walking out to the waterline without shoes or socks, and standing under the cry of the nightbirds, holding hands.

When they lay naked in bed together, lightbulb shining directly over them, he in her and both locked in restfulness after making love, he thought he saw her eyes screwed up with pain, until he realized it was the light from above shining through the strands and lines of her hair and reflecting them on the skin surrounding her closed eyes. The nights were becoming one night, days one day now that the holiday was ending. The children would remember the days, but they would only remember the nights. She felt the warm thickness of his shoulders and back, the relaxed flesh of his buttocks. It was all comfort, and love, and silence, and she wondered when it would break up into the violent colours of chaos, then smiled

84

at her pessimism and drew deeply on the hope that it never would.

'Happy, love?' he said, sensing it, never daring to ask if he knew she was not.

'Oh yes. You?'

They shifted on to their sides. 'Never more happy,' he told her. 'You know that.'

'I do.'

It was raining when they climbed into the train next day, a soft warm summer letdown from low cloud that made them happier than if they'd left the seaside with sun still shining. 'I'll save up,' he said, 'and we'll come again next year.'

'How many months is that?' Paul asked, digging his spade into the carriage floor.

Mark told him.

'How many weeks, then?'

'Fifty-odd.'

'How many minutes?'

He took out a biro and wrote on the margin of his *Daily Mirror*. 'Twenty-one thousand,' he laughed.

'I'll count them,' Paul said, as the train jerked and he fell against his mother.

The fence stood up, and so did the rosebush, every branch stem lined with concealed thorns among the remnants of decaying blossoms. More than a year had passed, and the sooty frost of winter lay over factories and houses. The factory covered more acreage than the houses. Across Ilkeston Road whole streets were cleared, a ground plan of cobbled laneways revealed. Blocks of flats, thin and high up the hill towards Canning Circus, stood like strands of hair stiffening at some apparition on the horizon that no human being could see because they were not made of concrete and girders, windows and seasoned wood. Such flats had now replaced the bucket-hovels that had held down the daisies for a hundred years, he thought, riding home on his way for dinner.

Home was where Jean and the children had once lived with her husband, and now allowed him to stay, though not in the man and wife sense, for his bed was in the parlour. 'I don't see why we can't share one bedroom,' he said.

'I do,' she retorted. 'I want some privacy in my life.'

Coming back to Nottingham after their sublime fortnight by the sea had the opposite effect to what he'd expected. The bliss of it seemed to have broken the back of their tenuous need for each other. Instead of the fabulous beginning of a full rich life together he now looked on their holiday as the height of affection and intimacy from which, through some unexplained perversity in Jean, they began to descend. Though not afraid to have the neighbours think they were living together, she seemed ashamed that she and Mark should actually do so.

At times she regretted having 'taken a lodger', useful and loving though he was. He was calm and tender, nothing upset him, neither the fact that his tea was late, nor the surge of kids jumping like mad things over him after an evening consumed in the sweat of overtime. He was goodness itself. Silver spoons must have been laid out for him at some time in his life, no matter what state he was born in. His goodness increased her feeling of guilt at having driven her husband away – though knowing in her heart that she was at least no more at fault than he had been.

Mark came home in the evening with a wide smile at the sight of her, and she tried to match him in it, would stand up from the table to greet him, while feeling desperately shy if the children were there. If they were out playing she would not even stand up. Because he was happy all of her moods were a torture to him. When he asked what was wrong, and she could not reply, it only proved that he was superfluous in the house.

'I'll go, then,' he said late one night.

She jumped up. 'No, don't Mark, don't.'

'What else can I do?'

'Stay, stay. I'd die if you left me.'

He held her. 'I don't want to go. My god I don't. I couldn't. But why aren't you happy, love?'

'You're too good,' she said, her tears wetting his close face. 'You're too good to me, Mark. I don't deserve this.'

'You do,' he said, fighting back a bleak inner weeping of his own. He questioned what she called his goodness, but it seemed no time to argue about that. 'You deserve any good thing that can happen to you,' he went on, pleading with her to accept whatever he had to give. But she went on crying, as if a moss-grown moon of despair had lodged itself in her heart that she had no hope of ever prising loose. It was hard to give comfort, impossible to reach her, but he stayed close and stroked her hair, saying that he loved her, loved her, thought she was beautiful, wonderful, the only woman of his life. But he felt empty, knew he was saying all this at the wrong time, that none of it was getting through, for she was beyond all aid and sympathy, untouchable. 'Leave me,' she moaned, 'leave me.'

'I can't. I never will.'

'Leave me alone. Go away.' It wasn't the first time she'd been so upset, but now it felt so bad that he thought his heart would burst, suffering so much himself at the manifestation of her grave unhappiness that he could in no way help her. She had so much, everything when you knew there was nothing further that she could attain or reach for.

Sometimes her sister came to look after the children and they went to see a good film, or walk around the streets talking and holding hands, going later into a pub to sit alone and lost in their own common glow. Every weekend they took the children either boating to Beeston Weir or for a picnic over Catstone Hill. He not only did his best for them, but enjoyed it so that he didn't seem to be doing anything at all. She sensed this, hoping that if he did put himself out he would perform miracles and make her life worth living after all. If she could not have everything, then the world was a desert in the depths of the night that could never be walked away from.

He was inadequate before her desolation. 'Don't be so upset, Jean. What is it? What can I do for you?'

The very fact of asking meant that he could do nothing. 'I don't know,' she said, 'I feel frightened all the time. Something's wrong, and I don't know what it is. I don't even know why I'm on this earth.'

'What does it matter? What do you want to know for? It doesn't bother me, not knowing.'

'I know it doesn't. That's why you're so good!' Her cries shook against the house, as if she were being deliberately tormented by some totally unfeeling person. But it was all coming from inside her, he thought, tightening his grip. The torture of helplessness passed on to him, the fact that his selfless love could do nothing to prevent the unexplained agony of her suffering – that he could not bear to be close to. It shook his heart to the core, and his own tears fell, filled with remorse because he could not follow Jean where some anguish he was not privileged to be part of had taken her right away from him.

They held each other tightly, sat on the floor, and wept aloud.

He got up one morning and fried an egg for breakfast. Jean did not go to work any more, and he took up a cup of tea before leaving.

A black dawn drizzle was falling outside, rattling against the loose window frame. It was a shame to sally into it, yet he liked going to work, being absorbed all day among noise and sawdust, fitting together unending rows of doors and windows. As labour it was less monotonous because he was now head man in the department, an unofficial foreman whose position was not yet confirmed by the management because they wanted to delay his increase in wages. But it would come, though he was already paying for it by having less jocular talks with his friends than before. Still, it was a better life, even if he did take a stint on actual chipping to make sure the quota was rushed out at the end of each day.

The stairs creaked under him as he went up with the tray. The children were staying for a week with her sister, and they had slept the last few nights together in her bed. 'I'm off to work,' he said, bending to her ear.

Her white shoulders and the pink straps of her nightdress shone under the bed light, dark long hair spreading back across the pillow. She opened her eyes, and saw his thin-faced smile turned on her, an expression of uncertainty because he was never sure in what sort of mood she was going to wake up. Their faces were like the two covers of a book, and when they pressed together everything was packed between them, and nothing got out. They kissed several times, rare for a morning. 'Did you sleep well?' he asked, pouring her tea.

'Right under,' she smiled.

'You'll feel better today, then.'

She thought how good his face was, how handsome and thin, full of intelligence and feeling and everything a woman might want and be happy living with. She was tranquil and happy. 'Don't go to work.'

'I can't let a drop of rain put me off,' he smiled.

'All right. Give me another kiss before you go.'

When he went home in the evening he saw from the yard-end that the blinds were down. The gate was padlocked and bolted against him. It was dusk, and a sharp fresh wind came between the houses as if to clean out the backyards. A radio played from the lit-up house next door. He stared, as if to penetrate the bricks, fixed in his own desperate musing. In a moment the lights would mushroom and he would hear the hollow voice of the television set, and when the lock dropped away from his cold fingers he would open the back door and see her sitting there in the warmth they had created for themselves.

A man and woman passed him in complete silence, and walked into a house further down the yard. He pushed at the gate as if to split its hinges. It held firm. Then his whole weight went against the fence, wanting to smash down every foot and paling of it. He grunted and moaned, pitting black strength at it till his shoulder felt cracked and shattered. It stood straight, unbendable. Looking into the garden he saw that the rosebush had rotted and withered right to the tips of its branches, but remembered it as beautiful, petals falling, a circle of leaves and pink spots on the soil.

He went to the neighbour's house and knocked at the door. 'Where's Jean, then?' he asked when the scullery light fell over him.

'I'm sorry,' Mrs Harby said. 'Her husband fetched her in a taxi this afternoon. She left your case here. Would you like a cup of tea?'

'Was there anything else?'

'I can soon make you a cup of tea if you'd like one.'

'No thanks.'

She pulled a letter from her apron pocket. 'There was this she asked me to give you. It's a shame, that's all I can say.'

He balanced the heavy case over the crossbar of his bike. Why had she gone, in such a way and without telling him? If he had talked to her she would never have done it. They could have loved each other for ever but, having gone to the threshold of a full and tolerable life, they had shied back from it. But he didn't know. You never did know, and he wondered whether you had to live without knowing all your life, and in wondering this he had some glimmer as to why she had blown up their world and left him.

He leaned his bike against a wall, and stood the case close by. Street lamps glowed up the sloping cobbled street. Nothing had ever seemed so completely finished. The hum of the factory swamped into him, a slight relief on the pain.

He went to another lamp post, and under its light tore the unopened letter into as many pieces as he had strength for, held them above his head, gripped them tight in his fist. When his arm ached, he spread all fingers. The wind snapped the scraps of paper away, up and into the darker air beyond the lamp light, as quickly as a hundred birds vanishing before snow comes. He stood there for some time, then clenched his fist again. After a while he walked on.

ENOCH'S TWO LETTERS

Enoch's parents parted in a singular way. He was eight years of age at the time.

It happened one morning after he had gone to school, so that he didn't know anything about it till coming home in the evening.

Jack Boden got up as usual at seven o'clock, and his wife, who was Enoch's mother, set a breakfast of bacon and egg before him. They never said much, and spoke even less on this particular morning, because both were solidly locked in their separate thoughts which, unknown to each other, they were at last intending to act on.

Instead of getting a bus to his foundry, Jack boarded one for the city centre. He sought out a public lavatory where, for the price of a penny, he was able to draw off his overalls, and emerge with them under his arm. They were wrapped in the brown paper which he had put into his pocket before leaving the house, a sly and unobtrusive movement as he called from the scullery: 'So long, love. See you this afternoon.'

Now wearing a reasonable suit, he walked to the railway station. There he met René, who had in her two suitcases a few of his possessions that he had fed to her during clandestine meetings over the past fortnight. Having worked in the same factory, they had, as many others who were employed there saw, 'fallen for each other'. René wasn't married, so there seemed nothing to stop her going away with him. And Jack's dull toothache of a conscience had, in the six months since knowing her, cured itself at last.

Yet they got on the train to London feeling somewhat alarmed at the step they had taken, though neither liked to say anything in case the other should think they wanted to back out. Hardly a word was spoken the whole way. René wondered what her parents would say when they saw she'd gone.

Jack thought mostly about Enoch, but he knew he'd be safe enough with his mother, and that she'd bring him up right. He would send her a letter from London to explain that he had gone – in case she hadn't noticed it.

No sooner had Jack left for his normal daylight stint at the foundry than his wife, Edna, attended to Enoch. She watched him eat, standing by the mantelshelf for a good view of him during her stare. He looked up, half out of his sleep, and didn't smile back at her.

She kissed him, pushed sixpence into his pocket, and sent him up the street to school, then went upstairs to decide what things to take with her. It wasn't a hard choice, for though they had plenty of possessions, little of it was movable. So it turned out that two suitcases and a handbag held all she wanted.

There was ample time, and she went downstairs to more tea and a proper breakfast. They'd been married ten years, and for seven at least she'd had enough. The trouble with Jack was that he'd let nothing worry him. He was so trustworthy and easy-going he got on her nerves. He didn't even seem interested in other women, and the worse thing about such a man was that he hardly ever noticed when you were upset. When he did, he accused you of upsetting him.

There were so many things wrong, that now she was about to leave she couldn't bring them to mind, and this irritated her, and made her think that it had been even worse than it was, rather than the other way round. As a couple they had given up tackling any differences between them by the human method of talking. It was as if the sight of each other struck them dumb. On first meeting, a dozen years ago, they had been unable to say much – which, in their mutual attraction, they had confused with love at first sight. And nowadays they didn't try to talk to each other about the way they felt any more because neither of them thought it would do any good.

96

Having come this far, the only thing left was to act. It wasn't that life was dull exactly, but they had nothing in common. If they had, maybe she could have put up with him, no matter how bad he was.

For a week she'd been trying to write a letter, to be posted from where she was going, but she couldn't get beyond: 'I'm leaving you for good, so stop bothering about me any more. Just look after Enoch, because I've had my bellyful and I'm off.' After re-reading it she put it back and clipped her handbag shut.

Having decided to act after years of thinking about it, she was now uncertain as to what she would do. A sister lived in Hull, so her first plan was to stay there till she found a job and a room. This was something to hang on to, and beyond it she didn't think. She'd just have to act again, and that was that. Once you started there was probably no stopping, she thought, not feeling too good about it now that the time had come.

An hour later she turned the clock to the wall, and walked out of the house for good, safe in knowing that shortly after Enoch came in from school his father would be home to feed him. They had lavished a lot of love on Enoch – she knew that – maybe too much, some of which they should have given to each other but had grown too mean and shy to.

She left the door unlocked so that he could just walk in. He was an intelligent lad, who'd be able to turn on the gas fire if he felt cold. When Mrs Mackley called from her back door to ask if she was going on her holidays, Edna laughed and said she was only off to see Jack's mother at Netherfield, to take some old rags that she needed to cut up and use for rug-clippings.

'Mam,' Enoch cried, going in by the back door. 'Mam, where's my tea?'

He'd come running down the road with a pocketful of marbles. His head in fact looked like one of the more psychedelic ones, with a pale round face, a lick of brilliant ginger hair down over his forehead, and a streak of red toffee-stain across his mouth.

Gossiping again, he thought scornfully, seeing the kitchen empty. He threw his coat, still with the sleeves twisted, over to the settee. The house did have more quiet than usual, he didn't know why. He turned the clock to face the right way, then went into the scullery and put the kettle on.

The tea wasn't like his mother made it. It was too weak. But it was hot, so he put a lot of sugar in to make up for it, then sat at the table to read a comic.

It was early spring, and as soon as it began to get dark he switched the light on and went to draw the curtains. One half came over easily, but the other only part of the way, leaving a foot-wide gap of dusk, like a long, open mouth going up instead of across. This bothered him for a while, until it got dark, when he decided to ignore it and switch the television on.

From hoping to see his mother, he began to wonder where his father was. If his mother had gone to Aunt Jenny's and missed the bus home, maybe his father at the foundry had had an accident and fallen into one of the moulds – from which it was impossible to get out alive, except as a skeleton.

Jam pot, butter dish, knife, and crumbs were spread over the kitchen table when he got himself something to eat. Not that it bothered him, that his father might have been killed, because when they had left him for an hour on his own a few months ago he had wondered what he would do if they never came back. Before he'd had time to decide, though, they had opened the door to tell him to get a sandwich and be off to bed sharp, otherwise he'd be too tired to get up for school in the morning. So he knew they'd be back sooner than he expected. When Johnny Bootle's father had been killed in a lorry last year he'd envied him, but Johnny Bootle himself hadn't liked it very much.

Whether they came back or not, it was nice being in the

house on his own. He was boss of it, could mash another pot of tea if he felt like it, and keep the gas fire burning as long as he liked. The telly was flickering but he didn't want to switch it off, even though heads kept rolling up and up, so that when he looked at it continually for half a minute it seemed as if they were going round in a circle. He turned to scoop a spoonful of raspberry jam from the pot, and swallow some more cold tea.

He sat in his father's chair by the fire, legs stretched across the rug, but ready to jump at the click of the outdoor latch, and be back at the table before they could get into the room. His father wouldn't like him being in his chair, unless he were sitting on his knee. All he needed was a cigarette, and though he looked on the sideboard and along the shelf there were none in sight. He had to content himself with trying to whistle in a thick manly style. Johnny Bootle had been lucky in his loss, because he'd had a sister.

If they didn't come back tonight he wouldn't go to school in the morning. They'd shout at him when they found out, but that didn't matter if they were dead. It was eight o'clock, and he wondered where they were. They ought to be back by now, and he began to regret that he'd hoped they never would be, as if God's punishment for thinking this might be that He'd never let them.

He yawned, and picked up the clock to wind it. That was what you did when you yawned after eight in the evening. If they didn't come soon he would have to go upstairs to bed, but he thought he would get some coats and sleep on the sofa down here, with the gas fire shining bright, rather than venture to his bedroom alone. They'd really gone for a night out, and that was a fact. Maybe they were late coming back because they'd gone for a divorce. When the same thing had happened to Tom Brunt it was because his mam had gone to fetch a baby, though he was taken into a neighbour's house next door before he'd been alone as long as this.

He looked along the shelf to see if he had missed a cigarette that he could put into his mouth and play at smoking with. He had good eyes and no need of glasses, that was true, because he'd been right first time. In spite of the bread and jam he still felt hungry, and went into the scullery for some cheese.

When the light went, taking the flickering telly with it, he found a torch at the back of the dresser drawer, then looked for a shilling to put in the meter. Fortunately the gas fire gave off enough pink glow for him to see the borders of the room, especially when he shone the torch beam continually around the walls as if it were a searchlight looking for enemy planes.

'It was a long wait to Tipperary' – as he had sometimes heard his father sing while drunk, but his eyes closed, with the piece of cheese still in his hands, and he hoped he would drop off before they came in so that they'd be sorry for staying out so late, and wouldn't be able to be mad at him for not having gone to bed.

He walked across the room to the coat hooks in the recess, but his mother's and father's coats had gone, as he should have known they would be, since neither of them was in. There was nothing to put over himself when he went to sleep, but he still wouldn't go upstairs for a blanket. It would be as bad as going into a wood at night. He had run across the road when a bus was coming, and seen Frankenstein once on the telly, but he wouldn't go into a wood at night, even though lying Jimmy Kemp claimed to have done so.

Pushing one corner at a time, he got the table back against the sideboard. There was an oval mirror above the mantel-shelf, and he leaned both elbows on it to get as good a look at himself as he could in the wavering pink light – his round face and small ears, chin in shadow, and eyes popping forward. He distorted his mouth with two fingers, and curled a tongue hideously up to his nose to try and frighten himself away from the bigger fear of the house that was threatening him with tears.

It was hard to remember what they'd done at school today, and when he tried to imagine his father walking into the house and switching on the light it was difficult to make out his face very clearly. He hated him for that, and hoped one day to kill him with an axe. Even his mother's face wasn't easy to bring back, but he didn't want to kill her. He felt his knee caps burning, being too close to the gas bars, so he stood away to let them go cool.

When he was busy rolling up the carpet in front of the fire, and being away from the mirror, his parents suddenly appeared to him properly, their faces side by side with absolute clarity, and he wished they'd come back. If they did, and asked what the bloody hell he thought he was doing rolling up the carpet, he'd say well what else do you expect me to do? I've got to use something for a blanket when I go to sleep on the settee, haven't I?

If there was one skill he was glad of, it was that he could tell the time. He'd only learned it properly six months ago, so it had come just right. You didn't have to put a shilling in the clock, so that was still ticking at least, except that it made him feel tired.

He heaved at the settee, to swivel it round in front of the fire, a feat which convinced him that one day he'd be as strong as his father – wherever he was. There was certainly no hope of the gas keeping on till the morning, so he turned it down to number two. Then he lay on the settee and pulled the carpet over him. It smelled of stone and pumice, and of soap that had gone bad.

He sniffed the cold air, and sensed there was daylight in it, though he couldn't open his eyes. Weaving his hand as far as it would go, he felt that the gas fire had gone out, meaning that the cooking stove wouldn't work. He wondered why his eyelids were stuck together, then thought of chopping up a chair to make a blaze, but the grate was blocked by the gas fire. This disappointed him, because it would have been nice to lean over it, warming himself as the bottom of the kettle got blacker and blacker till it boiled at the top.

When his eyes mysteriously opened, old Tinface the clock said it was half past seven. In any case there were no matches left to light anything. He went into the scullery to wash his face.

He had to be content with a cup of milk, and a spoon of sugar in it, with more bread and cheese. People were walking along the backyards on their way to work. If they've gone for good, he thought, I shall go to my grandma's, and I'll have to change schools because she lives at Netherfield, miles away.

His mother had given him sixpence for sweets the morning before, and he already had twopence, so he knew that this was enough to get him half fare to Netherfield.

That's all I can do, he thought, turning the clock to the wall, and wondering whether he ought to put the furniture right in case his parents came in and got mad that it was all over the place, though he hoped they wouldn't care, since they'd left him all night on his own.

Apart from not wanting to spend the sixpence his mother had given him till she came back, he was sorry at having to go to his grandma's because now he wouldn't be able to go to school and tell his mates that he'd been all night in a house on his own.

He pushed a way to the upper deck of the bus, from which height he could look down on the roofs of cars, and see level into the top seats of other buses passing them through the town. You never know, he thought, I might see 'em – going home to put a shilling each in the light and gas for me. He gave his money to the conductor.

It took a long time to get clear of traffic at Canning Circus, and he wished he'd packed up some bread and cheese before leaving the house. Men were smoking foul fags all around, and a gang of boys going to Peoples' College made a big noise until the conductor told them to stop it or he'd put them off.

He knew the name of his grandmother's street, but not how to get there from the bus stop. A postman pointed the direction for him. Netherfield was on the edge of Nottingham, and huge black cauliflower clouds with the sun locked inside came over on the wind from Colwick Woods.

When his grandmother opened the back door he was turning the handle of the old mangle outside. She told him to stop it, and then asked in a tone of surprise what had brought him there at that time of the morning.

'Dad and mam have gone,' he said.

'Gone?' she cried, pulling him into the scullery. 'What do you mean?' He saw the big coal fire, and smelled the remains of bacon that she must have done for Tom's breakfast – the last of her sons living there. His face was distorted with pain. 'No,' she said, 'nay, you mustn't cry. Whatever's the matter for you to cry like that?'

The tea she poured was hot, strong, and sweet, and he was sorry at having cried in front of her. 'All right, now?' she said, drawing back to watch him and see if it was.

He nodded. 'I slept on the couch.'

'The whole night! And where can they be?'

He saw she was worried. 'They had an accident,' he told her, pouring his tea into the saucer to cool it. She fried him an egg, and gave him some bread and butter.

'Our Jack's never had an accident,' she said grimly.

'If they're dead, grandma, can I live with you?'

'Aye, you can. But they're not, so you needn't worry your little eyes.'

'They must be,' he told her, feeling certain about it.

'We'll see,' she said. 'When I've cleaned up a bit, we'll go and find out what got into 'em.' He watched her sweeping the room, then stood in the doorway as she knelt down to scrub the scullery floor, a smell of cold water and pumice when she reached the doorstep. 'I've got to keep the place spotless,' she said with a laugh, standing up, 'or your Uncle Tom would leave home. He's bound to get married one day though, and that's a fact. His three brothers did, one of 'em being your daft father.'

She held his hand back to the bus stop. If Uncle Tom does clear off it looks like she'll have me to look after. It seemed years already since he'd last seen his mother and father, and he was growing to like the adventure of it, provided they didn't stay away too long. It was rare going twice across town in one day.

It started to rain, so they stood in a shop doorway to wait for the bus. There wasn't so many people on it this time, and they sat on the bottom deck because his grandma didn't feel like climbing all them steps. 'Did you lock the door behind you?'

'I forgot.'

'Let's hope nobody goes in.'

'There was no light left,' he said. 'Nor any gas, I was cold when I woke up.'

'I'm sure you was,' she said. 'But you're a big lad now. You should have gone to a neighbour's house. They'd have given you some tea. Mrs Upton would, I'm sure. Or Mrs Mackley.'

'I kept thinking *they'd* be back any minute.'

'You always have to go to the neighbours,' she told him, when they got off the bus and walked across Ilkeston Road. Her hand had warmed up now from the pumice and cold water. 'Don't kick your feet like that.'

If it happened again, he would take her advice. He hoped it wouldn't, though next time he'd sleep in his bed and not be frightened.

They walked down the yard, and in by the back door. Nothing was missing, he could have told anybody that, though he didn't speak. The empty house seemed dead, and he didn't like that. He couldn't stay on his own, so followed his grandmother upstairs and into every room, half expecting her to find them in some secret place he'd never known of.

The beds were made, and wardrobe doors closed. One of the windows was open a few inches, so she slammed it shut and locked it. 'Come on down. There's nowt up here.'

She put a shilling in the gas meter, and set a kettle on the stove. 'Might as well have a cup of tea while I think this one out. A bloody big one it is, as well.'

It was the first time he'd heard her swear, but then, he'd never seen her worried, either. It made him feel better. She thought about the front room, and he followed her.

'They kept the house clean, any road up,' she said, touching the curtains and chair covers. 'That's summat to be said for 'em. But it ain't everything.'

'It ain't,' he agreed, and saw two letters lying on the mat just inside the front door. He watched her broad back as she bent to pick them up, thinking now that they were both dead for sure.

THE VIEW

They were bringing another body into the churchyard.

He had a simple view of it from the balcony of his three-roomed council flat. Grass was flattened by frost, streaks of powdered dew, like hair that had turned grey overnight because it was so cold. Inside the living room a coal fire blazed, while outside, across the paved lane and beyond the churchyard wall, a dozen people filed between headstones towards a hole already prepared for whoever it was they were carrying in today.

It was the first frost of the year, and from now until the softening break of spring the grave-digger's life, like everybody else's in these Nottinghamshire hills, would be a hard one. Through the last eight years Jack had seen many people buried from the view point of his balcony. Holes were excavated by the patient slow old man who seemed, like those about to occupy the place he dug, to have all the time in the world. Jack had seen people come with wreaths and set them down carefully. Later they'd scatter the flowers, or stand at the tap near the gate with urns to fill with fresh jonquils bought in Worksop market or grown in their own home gardens.

He'd seen it all by accident, on idly glancing out of the window when tired of reading the paper or watching the telly. Other people on the estate didn't get this grandstand vista, and he thought they were slightly deprived. This constant picture of burial and the blood's end made his own life seem longer, as if he'd already done that trip into the churchyard, been carried in and had the soil tipped down and stamped over him.

He laughed. No fear. If and when he did die he'd want no Christian graveyard interment, or whatever they called it. As far as he was concerned they could throw his body on the nearest ash tip or cart it off to a hospital in case something could be learned from it. You never know, though there were no 'physical peculiarities' he was aware of.

A thin sun made a spreading blister in the clouds. The group surrounding the oblong hole ruffled a bit, like a big dark bird trying to get its feathers back into shape. He could only see one corner of the coffin, which slipped from sight as if the dead man's friends around it had had the ropes pulled out of their frozen grasp. They had been like statues and would have held it there for ever. It occurred to him to wonder why he thought it was a man who was being buried. He smiled about it.

The sun went back, having seen enough. The people moved along the path towards the church gate. The vicar's black vestments flapped in the breeze of his legs. He had once knocked at Jack's door to ask in a grimly bright manner for a weekly donation to the upcost of his church, but his reception had been as icy as the soil now swinging in clods from the spade of the gravedigger, who worked to keep warm and fill in the gaps around the coffin.

He went in to get his tea.

He washed the tomatoes, sliced the brawn, and unwrapped the sponge-cake. Sometimes he witnessed a wedding from the church, which made him feel older than when he saw a burial. After Lent it was a weekly show his wife looked forward to, and sometimes he might deign to watch with her. His sardonic comments didn't cut down her sentimental pleasure at the sight of so many cars, so much white brocade and confetti, though she flushed at knowing that each remark was meant to destroy the pledge of their own wedding that had taken place at the same church before these flats were built and before anyone had been able to gloat on it from where he gloated now.

That was ten years ago. Not only had so much water flowed by since then, but the actual bridges had been pushed down and swept away. In fact the river-bed was dry, and its banks cracking in the heat. He told himself that the fire of a too bitter and passionate sun had turned them as dry as that dust on the moon that the American space ships scooped up.

He sliced a carving knife through the middle of the tomato, swallowed one side and contemplated each neat seed in its allotted place of the other. While he was at work making horseshoes, and ornamental gates when that trade was slack, she indulged in the eternal round of domestic bullshit, keeping the house especially clean so that she could tell him off about dirtying it as soon as he came in through that door. Women aren't good for much, except having kids. That was all they were allowed to do, most of 'em, though *they'd* not got any yet.

He'd left an Ellery Queen magazine in the bedroom and went through to get it. It smelt cold in there, sharp against his nose, and he thought of lighting the gas fire to tone the chill down a bit in time for them going to bed. There was no telling when she'd be back though. A girl had come round for her, telling them her mother had had a stroke, so maybe it wouldn't be for a while yet. If it was bad he'd be at a funeral himself in a day or two, instead of watching it from his usual perch by the window.

Getting up from the gas fire to put the match-end in the ash-tray on his wife's dressing table, he noted the few hairpins and pots of cream in front of the swivel mirror. By the side, and never out of her sight, was a large coloured photo of her favourite pop star which she brought from her own bedroom at home when they got married. He hated it at first, though only joked about it, and didn't push that too far when he saw how much his teasing upset her. He no longer minded her being in love with it or him, as she'd hinted often enough, for who could bother about such a weak and pretty face as that?

He heard her coming up the steps, so opened the door before she could put her key in the lock. She looked worried and flushed, yet smiled at him nevertheless. There was no doubt to either of them that she was glad to be back.

She took off her coat with the fur collar, and rubbed her hands before the fire. 'I'm glad you kept it going. I know you can always be relied on for that.'

He looked at her, glad indeed she was home. She was a tall woman of thirty, who had been buxom but was now thinning at the face. He'd worried about her losing weight, and sent her to the doctor, who told her to drink a bottle of stout every day and eat more – and to come again if she went on losing. She hadn't, and had even put on a pound or two in the last week, so worried now because she didn't want to get back to the weight she had had before, which she'd considered was too much.

'How was your mam, then?'

'Not too bad. She might be better in a month or two, so the doctor said. Dad looks worse than her, fretting so much.'

'They'll have to let me know if there's owt I can do,' he said.

She kissed him, and he held her: 'I've put the fire on in the bedroom.'

'Lovely,' she said. The smell of her face encouraged him to reach round and kiss behind her neck, carefully lifting up the broad tail of her hair to get at it. After a while she said: 'I'll cook you some supper,' and went into the kitchen.

'I had bread and tomato already.'

'That's not supper,' she said. 'I'll do that steak and put some taters on.' He tried to say it was all right and not to bother, but she pulled pans out of the cupboard and set to work. 'What were you doing with yourself, love?' she asked, as he stood in the doorway to enjoy the sight of her.

'Read a bit, then watched some poor sod getting buried. Better than telly!'

'It was Mr Jones,' she said, solemnly. 'Albert Jones. He was eighty-five. Dad remembered working under him as a lad.

112

People live a long time round here. If you pass twenty you'll get to be a hundred, they say.'

Maybe it had depressed him, watching the burial that afternoon. 'Not me, though.'

She looked at him, a potato in one hand and a knife in the other. 'Are you trying to upset me, Jack? I think I've had enough for one day.'

'Never!' he laughed, and she noticed how happy it made him look, though he felt there was some truth in what he'd said.

'If owt happened to you I'd die myself,' she said tenderly. 'I'd go off my head. You're the only man there'll ever be in my life, I do know that much.'

He didn't doubt that she loved him, and cursed himself for his selfish and unguarded remark. He didn't know what made him come out with it, though at the same time he felt much better for having done so.

It came back to her a few weeks later when he was killed at work. He was standing outside examining an iron gate he'd sweated on for nearly a week, checking it for faults. A three-ton lorry backed into him, ramming the heavy bars and crushing him against the wall.

When they buried him she knew, through the piercing grief of her tears, that this was one funeral he wouldn't look at from his favourite chair by the window. She'd rather it was anybody but him in the box, about to be lowered into the earth.

Her father led her to the car, for her mother was still too badly to get out. On the way back it started to snow, and she knew she'd never be able to see snow again without thinking of him, unable to understand why such a wicked blow should have been aimed at her.

Everyone thought a job would take her mind off it. 'You've got to live,' they said. 'You're a young woman and have your whole life in front of you.' Which she knew was true. She was losing so much weight over it that she had to get out a bit more into the world and make a few friends.

At the supermarket she met a young man whom she thought looked very much like the pop star photo on her dressing table. She'd wanted to take this photo off now that Jack was gone, but her hand just wouldn't reach out to unclip the back and tear it up. She saw later that it had kept her from breaking down altogether, and here was this man who looked so much like the face on it that she couldn't believe it when she first saw him come out of the office and walk across to ask her for the day's accounts.

She soon put on fourteen pounds, and was once more the tall buxom woman she'd been a year before. Lines had gone from her face, and her smile was back – more brightly than before, said her mother. It was impossible that she'd ever go out with this young man, but she looked at him so much and hard, as if she'd known him for ten years, that the quiet familiarity in her expression began to intrigue him.

When he shyly and quietly asked her to go for a drink one night she didn't even seem surprised. He wasn't the sort of man Jack would have much time for, would have made fun of him and called him mardy and girlish. But Jack wasn't here any more and, as everybody had said, she had to go on living after all.

When she brought him home a few weeks later, back to the flat where she'd lived so long and happily with Jack, she made him a cup of coffee in the kitchen. She then cut him some bread and cheese, apologizing for not cooking a proper meal.

They'd taken off their coats in the living room, and in his stroll around it he noticed the view over the cemetery. 'What a place to live!' he said. 'I'd be dead miserable if I had to look at that every day.'

She shuddered at his bad joke, but refused to get upset

about it. 'Well, you can't tell the council where to put up their flats.'

'No,' he said, stroking his wispy moustache as he gave the graveyard one more contemptuous glance across the summery dusk, 'but you can move.'

While he ate she went through to the bedroom and quickly tore up the photograph of her favourite pop star. There was a vivid smile on her face as she chucked the pieces on to the still burning coal fire in the living room. Jack's photo stayed on her dressing table, for she couldn't touch that, ever. When she married Peter, as they were now promised to do, it would stay in its appointed place.

A TRIP TO SOUTHWELL

Alec leaned from the window of the empty compartment to fix the time by the platform clock.

Even if she ran down the stone stairs in her click-heelers shouting for him to stop he'd shrug and turn away with a slit-grin that would grip the heart painfully – knowing there was no chance of her coming whatever he felt or hoped.

At the age of seventeen, if you fall in love with a girl younger than yourself, you don't know what you're letting yourself in for. It pulled you to the middle of the earth and was hard to get out of once you were that far down. There was so much honey you got stuck like any black and orange bee. When you weren't gassed with sweetness your feet got burned.

To begin with he hadn't even known he was in love, and she was still fifteen, what's more. Things shifted under you like on the cakewalk at Goose Fair, but it had always been like that with him, and he expected it never to alter. If he hadn't lived in Nottingham he wouldn't have met her, which might have been for the best. When things went wrong what could you do except wish they hadn't happened?

Then his old man got a better-paid job managing a butcher's shop in Leicester instead of cutting up chops and joints under somebody else down Radford. But you couldn't blame him for the break-up no more than you could for getting me in the world in the first place. So they moved, and there he was as well, or would be (and for good) when the train got there in forty minutes – time enough to go back over the whole tormenting issue.

Everybody was het-up after spilling from the late-night pictures, and the distant smell of a fish-and-chip shop came through the thick and icy fog. Alec saw her standing apart from her sister and saying nothing, while noise from the rest of them clattered around the lamp post.

The best compliment you could make in those days was that somebody was 'quiet'. He once heard Doris Mackin say a boy named Bernard was smashing because he talked so quiet. Well, when he saw Mavis Hallam, and heard her reply to her sister who called out to come and join the gang, he thought how marvellous that her voice was soft.

Even though it was quiet he heard her say: 'I don't want to, our Helen. We'll have to be going soon, or dad'll shout at us when he sees us coming in late' – as if shouting was the worst punishment anybody could have, and that they should do anything to avoid it.

'Don't be daft,' Helen called, punching Bill Cotgrave who tried to get too much out of her: 'We aren't even courting,' she bawled at him, 'so get your scabby 'ands off of me.'

Mavis turned without answering, and sensed Alec looking at her. While he thought of what to say, in an equally low voice if he could manage it, he remembered that her softened tone was nevertheless a bit sarcastic. Though not lost on him, it didn't matter at a time when he'd give his right arm to know more about her.

Joshing and laughing the whole gang turned from the lamp post and straggled up Berridge Road. The world had divided into moving through the dark mist, and the quiet presence of Mavis who came on not far behind.

Between the two, Alec surmised that even though she lagged out of sight, and in spite of her soft voice and sarky tone, she still wanted to mill in with the rest. There was much of that in him too. Larking about bored him, and he didn't go for the dirty jokes and swinging hands (though he thought he could hold his own with both), yet he was glad to put up with it for the palliness and warmth. Bill Cotgrave and Alf Meggison worked at the same electrical firm, and with them Alec went twice a week to the youth club, completing a triangle of home, work, and leisure.

He waited for her. 'Why don't you catch up?'

'Why don't *you*?' she asked, quiet and unhurried, and close enough for him to see her smile.

'I wanted to drop back a bit and talk.'

'Talk, then.'

He tried to hold her hand, but she pulled it away.

'If that's how it is,' he said.

'I said talk, not grab. I don't know you that well.'

She didn't raise her voice through this, or even sound harsh, which made him want all the more to hold her. He saw it was going to be a long job, especially after this rebuff, and what he thought of as his first mistake.

He'd only seen her a couple of times, because Helen, her elder sister, didn't consider her old enough to mix with the rough and tumble she herself kept. A couple of the lads had already 'had it' with Helen, but he couldn't ever see himself getting on the same track with Mavis – though you never know how things might turn out. He felt something more than that towards her, and didn't know what it was, unable to put it down to her soft voice, which would be too easy.

'Anyway,' she said, pushing the silence away, 'I don't know whether I like people with ginger hair.'

She was the first who'd ever objected to it, which he supposed was something else that made her different. 'I've got blue eyes,' he said. 'I expect they put your back up as well. I'll dye 'em if you like. If I'm too tall for you I'll take a correspondence course in shrinking. Maybe I could even do it at night school.'

Her laugh was more an attempt at one, though he liked her for it because it showed he was on the right track. He'd never seen her properly in broad day or electric light, always in the shifting flicker of a street lamp or the dim colours outside a cinema, and he longed now, searching for the wit to make her laugh properly, to see her clearly.

He had a fair idea of what she looked like, but being unsure of himself he wondered, if he met her in the possible sunlight of tomorrow's mid-day walking along the street and wearing a different coat, whether he'd be able to tell her well enough to risk saying hello Mavis and how are you?

Going to the pictures once, on his own, he got talking to a girl inside, and before the end they were kissing as if they'd known each other six weeks. Afterwards, her mother was outside to see her home, but they'd already arranged another meeting. In the following days he forgot what she looked like, not knowing whether she was tall or short or fair or dark – or anything whatever about her appearance. It might even have been a matter of conjecture whether or not she had a wooden leg, for all he noticed.

When the time came he approached the only other girl outside the cinema, and almost got into a fight because her boyfriend who had just dropped off a bus thought he was bothering her. He went up to several girls in the next half hour, none of whom was the dated one, though he would have gone in with any who said they were. He thought he was going off his head, but told himself that life was like that. When the right girl turned up he spotted her straight away.

He would know Mavis, however, not so much from her distinct features as from a feeling of her presence that would bring instant recognition. He felt more than saw her slightly plump figure and long coat, her head held back, and short black curly hair, her small curved mouth and full cheeks, shapely ears and pale skin. She wore no make-up, as if to emphasize the fact of not mixing in. There was no taint or smell to disguise any part of her, which he supposed was due to her being only fifteen (though sixteen in a fortnight, she said) and made him think that if he got off with her he'd hear his pals yelling he was a cradle-snatcher, since he himself was already seventeen.

'I've known you long enough,' he answered, which sounded

too much like a jocular complaint that one of his mates might use, and one he'd often put on with other girls. Since her voice was softly controlled he imagined she was repeating this in her mind and laughing at him, so he went on to make it worse – trying to forget what an older man at work once said: that ginger-nuts often thought people were laughing at them when they weren't. 'I'll meet you Sunday afternoon if you like, and we can go to Sunday School together.'

She missed his clumsy joke, and said: 'I've never been to such a place. In any case I wouldn't go with you. People'd know your sort a mile off – two miles, in fact.'

He felt better that she'd already gone to the trouble of putting him into a 'sort', though he realized this couldn't have been very difficult. 'What is my sort, anyway?' He managed to keep his voice as soft as hers, but only when asking questions.

'Always after the girls,' she scorned. 'Johnny Wiley told me about you.'

He wondered how Johnny Wiley had ever got close enough to tell her anything she'd listen to from a bastard like him. 'The world's full of big mouths,' he answered, gritting his teeth at being jealous so early on. 'People have dirty minds, that's all I can say.'

'He knows a thing or two, though, Johnny Wiley.'

'I'm not going out with anybody,' he told her. They walked side by side, and she didn't seem to mind. To make an impression he had to spill an interesting piece of news or gossip, as Johnny Wiley had done. Then maybe she'd remember it, and repeat that too. It would be one sort of step forward at least. 'I went out with Doreen Buckle, but we got fed up with each other. Her old man came back early from the pub and caught us in the house alone. We was only watching the box. But he put a stop to it. You know how it is.'

'That was her excuse,' Mavis said. 'She made up lies for all I know. But she blabbed out to everybody that *she* got fed up with *you.*'

He knew he should have spun off some lurid and filthy tale about Johnny Wiley, instead of telling her about his own dull self, both to get his revenge and to make her more interested in him. But he hadn't thought to lie, because it didn't seem necessary. Even if it was he wouldn't bother. Some people were too idle to tell lies, and he felt this was true of him.

But he was narked by the accuracy of her news: 'Why do they spill it all to you?'

She didn't respond, and he thought they confided so much in her because they never imagined she'd repeat what they said – with that quiet way of hers. Or she was so young they got kicks out of shocking her. He hadn't noticed that she had that sort of face, but the idea began to intrigue him. On the other hand, maybe her soft voice brought it out of them. 'I ought to keep my trap shut,' he added, putting an arm around her.

'You can if you like,' she said, meaning it would make no difference. 'We'd better get a move on or we won't catch the others up.'

'Not that I want to.'

'I do,' she jibed, 'with you hanging round me.' But she didn't shake his arm off, nor walk more quickly when the gang in front flowed round a corner.

Meeting her towards the end of a rainy winter they went to a snack bar and ate cheese cobs with a cup of coffee.

The place was empty but for them, which made her less shy than if it'd been full. But it was the first time he'd got her so much on her own, and he could see she was uneasy about it. He wondered if that was why he liked her, for if she was nervous there was something worth getting to know, especially when she spoke softly as well. Other such girls, he'd found, were often pan-mouths, shouting and snapping all around the place, and that sort could go and jump over a high wall with glass on top as far as he was concerned.

Mavis ate her cheese cob and said nothing, and that was the trouble because being so quiet it was up to him to talk, and he'd never been very good at that, especially with girls. So trust him to fall for one that needed the lipwork from him. But he hoped she might improve one day, and that the odds would equalize.

'Cob all right, duck?'

She wiped a crumb from her mouth. 'I'm not hungry, but it tastes good. I like not eating at home for a change. They tease me summat rotten, just because I'm the youngest. I'm fed up of it.'

That's why she's quiet and hangs back. Never gets a word in edgeways because she can't stand being chaffed. 'We'll go out and have a proper dinner some-time,' he said. 'I know a nice cafe up Pelham Street.'

'We could do,' she smiled.

He told her about his father getting ready to move to Leicester, which meant he'd be shifting that way as well.

'When's this?' she asked.

'In a couple of months.'

'There's no castle at Leicester,' she said.

'What difference does that make?'

'Nor a river, either.'

'So what?'

'It ain't got no middle then, has it?'

'Know-all!' he laughed. 'When did you go there? I've never seen you down there.'

'That's what everybody says.'

'You don't believe everybody, do you?' he scorned.

'It's not as good as Nottingham, I'm sure.'

She took his move more seriously than necessary, as if weighing up the points of living there herself. Then he knew he was imagining things. You always did if something was too good to be true. But it frightened him a bit, so he got back to reality: 'Anybody'd think it was my fault Leicester wasn't up to much.'

Maybe it wasn't. His father had snapped up the chance to go there, not only for a better job, but because Alec's sister had got pregnant. A change of place would stop all talk about her, and get her away from the man who was still pestering her but couldn't marry her because he'd already got a wife and kids of his own.

Mavis didn't answer. Nothing was his fault; nothing was her fault. Getting her into a café and away from the others meant he could sit opposite and take his time seeing her plain. You had to see somebody like that before you could view them in any way at all, and when you did see them clear you could tell whether there was anything there or not. It was hard to do outside because she was mostly in shadow or never still, or the others were jumping around and pulling at them to go here or there. And while kissing, they were too close to see each other.

He'd known his sister was pregnant even before his parents twigged it. A certain warmth came into her, a particular and not unpleasant smell as he passed her, plus a sudden weariness in her eyes at something like terror as she tried to subdue a good feeling she felt might gain the upper hand but ought not to.

He watched Mavis. Her lids were heavy and her eyes looked down, her lips still but always as if about to break into the smallest of sly smiles. Yet at the same time it seemed as if her face were made of stone.

It stopped raining, so they walked down Alfreton Road. He put his arm over her back and around her waist, noticing how small she was. Other girls had latched their arm about him as well at this stage, but Mavis didn't, emphasizing perhaps that with her it was no game, rather some sort of going out together that might have more seriousness in it. He realized with an inner laugh how hope latched on to nothing.

126

'I suppose you'll be away for good,' she said, 'when you go to Leicester.'

'I expect so. But it's a stone's throw. I went there on my bike a couple of months ago, and it only took two hours.'

She laughed in a way he didn't like, and wasn't meant to. 'You aren't going to come on your bike and see me, are you? All that way!'

'There's a train. A bike 'ud be handy if I missed the last one, though.'

'Don't worry,' she said, 'that wain't happen. It'll be funny – if you do come to see me on a bike.'

There were times when he just couldn't fathom her, when she wasn't friendly and made him wonder why she bothered to meet him in the first place. It seemed the world glittered so much for her that a bike was old-fashioned and out of place, like a horse-and-cart on a motorway.

The only test was when he tried to kiss her a few doors up from where she lived. The first time he'd got nothing out of her, but now the kiss was good and sweet, as if she'd been dreading it but liked it when it came.

She let him have most when on the back row of the Saturday-night pictures, where it was all right because nobody could see them. It was the only time she showed a bit of passion, and didn't always shift his hand when he put it under her coat and over her breasts. But the further they went together in the cinema the cooler she was when they got outside.

Now that he'd broken the ice all the lads of the gang were after her, whereas a month ago she'd been too young and remote and set apart to bother with, protected by her sister and her own quiet scorn. At the club Pete Whatton would come up behind and try to kiss her, or make a grab for her in other places. But the uproar from her sister stopped it, drowning the words that Mavis quietly spat back. If Alec was there he bumped Pete or anybody else away, threatening to blaze a red trail with them across town.

So Mavis, now desired, stood her ground among them, and knowing she was safe from all and sundry gave her face a livelier look, an expression that made the kisses for Alec more than marvellous because they were for him alone, though there wasn't always the warmth behind them that he would have liked.

They got on a bus and went up Trent valley to Southwell. Why he took her there he didn't know. He'd never been himself, had merely seen it marked on his brother's one-inch walking map and thought it a good place to make arrangements for since it seemed to be out in the country among lots of fields.

The bus called at villages along the river, and though spring was far on by the calendar it was only just coming in fact, water at half-flood lifting the edge of its leaden grey line up towards the narrow road, a cold wind flapping from the opposite direction unable to beat it back. Darkly packed trees on the other side went right up the steep line of hills, and he wished they'd gone that way instead, where the cover seemed better.

They walked from the bus stop back to the Minster, which he felt they must look into because he'd often heard about it. He'd never bothered with churches, yet liked the look of this one, possibly because Mavis was with him, a reason that made him feel stupid, as if threatening him with something he not only didn't understand but also disliked.

'*That's* an old gravestone,' she said, when they were in the churchyard. She took his hand. 'It's worn already, and he wasn't buried more than sixty years ago.'

'Look at this one then: he was only twenty-four. Gives me another seven years!'

'Cheerful,' she said. 'I want somebody who's going to last.'

'Don't worry about that, duck! I'll live to be a hundred.'

'All right, *duck*,' she mocked. He'd only said it in fun, but noticed how she often used his own jokes, which she pretended not to understand, just to get back at him.

He liked the Minster, pleased it wasn't a city church but one placed on its own, an island among green lawns. You could walk all round it, see every angle of its middle tower and two end pinnacles.

'Are you going in then, or aren't you?' she said with a smile, as if he needed dragging through the door.

'Can I carry you across the threshold?'

'We aren't going to live in it, dope! Anyway, you'd drop me.'

'Yes,' he said, holding the wooden door open for her, 'it's a lovely hard floor!'

They walked around the walls, a few feet apart. He saw how the sun shone through the small panes of plain windows. Other people were about, but far off down the nave. He went quietly behind and tried to kiss her.

'Stop it.' She swung away more quickly than he thought necessary. 'We're in a church.'

'It's all right. I've never been christened.'

'Leave me alone,' she hissed, buttoning her coat against the cold.

He felt stalled and irritated, though this feeling went when they strolled into the Chapter House. He reached it first, and stood by himself. He knew it was a beautiful place, the round room and arched ceiling, built so cleverly he couldn't think how and soon stopped trying to. Looking up and out of the small windows of plain glass he could see the indistinct shapes of the rest of the cathedral, clouds floating by in the light of the sky, like some magic scene which he knew was particular to the spot where he stood.

Mavis walked around the room, looking at each wooden seat specially built for the prelates of the neighbouring parishes. He read them aloud as he walked, feeling flippant now that Mavis had come into the room. He sat on a seat that had no village name: 'They must have kept this one for me!'

She was about to smile at his antic, but her expression changed to one of fury. 'Get up,' she cried.

'What?'

'Why don't you get up?'

He was puzzled at her rage. 'I like it. It fits me.'

'Somebody'll see you.'

'I've got as much right to sit in it as anybody,' he retorted.

'You're the end,' she said. 'Mocking things.'

She walked out quickly, ahead of him.

He caught her up at the door. 'I'm not serious. It was only a bit of fun.'

She smiled when they were in the sunlight. 'It's a nice church.'

Her bad mood had vanished.

'It is,' he agreed, taking her arm, and sweating inwardly because you never knew where you were with her.

They bought two Mars bars and walked into the fields. The grass was dark and rich, but cold looking.

'We went biking last year,' she said, 'and you should have seen the things that went on. It was hot, and Whitsun. We ate our stuff up Gotham Hills, and must have stayed a couple of hours. I was bored but they wouldn't come away. Everybody was in the bushes except me.'

He laughed. 'I wish I'd been there. Then we could have taken a turn. Just for a lie down. You need a bit of rest after biking out from Nottingham.'

'Our Helen had it off Johnny Wiley.'

'How do you know?'

She took the Mars bar from her pocket, peeled off the paper, and bit a third of it away. 'You could tell, that's all.' Then she wrapped up the rest and put it back for later. 'The way they crept out . . . They could hardly bike home.'

'You don't miss much, do you?' The tone of her voice

hadn't indicated whether she was telling it as a hint not to do anything like that with her, or whether she was trying to work herself into letting him do as he wanted.

It was hard to say, when you weren't sure what was in the offing, so they walked without talking. He cursed himself for his silence, knowing she thought he'd taken her tale as a warning. Wanting to break it, but unable to, made him feel worse. There were things to say but his mouth was full of concrete. He'd expected this before coming on the trip, and all week he'd been storing tales in his mind to tell her, but now he'd forgotten them.

The sun came out. He took her hand and it was warm, slightly sticky from the sweets she had eaten.

'Maybe we'll go biking at Easter,' he said. 'Just the two of us. I can't stand going in a big crowd with all the others.'

'I've got an aunt at Blidworth,' she told him. 'We could ride up there. It's not far, but it's hard in a wind. She might give us a piece of cake. She makes ever such good cake.'

'I went to Worksop last year,' he said, to prove it wasn't beyond him. 'Twenty-seven miles, each way. Coming back I got a puncture and there was still twelve miles to get home.'

He stopped talking, to find a way for them through a hedge. A twig stuck up his sleeve, and he pulled it free.

'Anyway, I thought I'd better mend it, and called at a farm to ask for a bowl of water so's I could find the bubble in the inner tube.'

'You aren't back'ards at coming forward.'

'She was a nice woman, and put one outside for me. Had an apron on and wore glasses. Even gave me a cup of tea after I'd fixed it up.'

'I expect there was a lot of sugar in it,' she said, tartly.

'Stacks. Sweet as honey.'

They stopped near the hill top, a straight line of dark wood in front. 'Nearly as sweet as you are.' When he kissed her she held herself stiffly.

'Don't you like it?' He sifted through his past life for another story to tell.

She said: 'Don't be daft' in such a way he was no wiser, but he kissed her again till she slipped aside and said they ought to get on or they'd be seen. You never knew who was chiking around.

The field was empty, and he couldn't see anything except green stubble, and sky with the odd hole of blue in it, blue flame drawing itself out and pulling more behind. It made him dizzy to look too long. It was a queer feeling, because though you felt alone in an empty field you couldn't be sure that the hedges surrounding it weren't filled with people. He disliked her mood leaping over on to him, having noticed how skilled she was at giving it a push.

There was no wind to disturb them, but she trod warily into the wood – as if afraid of snakes or toadstools. 'I don't know why you're bringing me here. There aren't any bluebells yet.'

'Are you frightened of being seen?'

'Course not.'

Her sharp denial told him that she was, yet it annoyed him that he couldn't finally be sure what unease was gripping her. 'Where *else* can we go? It's a change from the field. Would you like to live in the country?'

The path was muddy in places, and he guided her to the drier ridges. 'It's all right for an outing,' she said. 'I like pavements best.' It was green and dark, with a strong smell of soft bark and rotting ferns, soil, and hidden water. 'Let's get out of it.'

Like a good city dweller he'd noted the way in, and soon they were on the lane going downhill. There was a brook at the bottom, and it was hard getting her across. Being sarcastic and quiet of voice, and so cool towards him he thought she was the same with everyone else, she was finally physically timid when it came to distances, and brooks, and going into woods.

When he kissed her on the other side she clung to him. He was surprised and glad, and thought he was getting somewhere at last, but tried not to think of it in this way because it didn't tally with the holier feeling of love that swept in and took him over. Her body was hot through both their coats, and her kisses so firm it was difficult to get breath.

They walked towards a hedge and lay on his mackintosh in the driest part, grappling with such force they could not even kiss, clinging as if falling down through space and terrified at the impact that was coming soon.

They caught the bus from Thurgarton, and the city lights were on by the time it dragged up Carlton Hill. She sat on the inside seat, arm in his and head on his shoulder.

There was no doubt they loved each other, and though she hadn't exactly said so while they were by that hedge, he himself had murmured it a dozen times – which seemed to make up for it. He nevertheless wondered whether she hadn't held him so fiercely because such a grip would stop her getting the words out, though words, he knew, pushing his misgivings away at the expense of his better judgement, could not express everything. You had to take account, when all was said and done, of how people acted and the feelings shown that could never be mistaken.

They had lain by the hedge for a couple of hours, hands roaming at every part of each other, though they hadn't, as the gang phrase went, 'had it'. Because of this the sweet passion still lingering between them was more like real love than when he'd gone all the way with other girls.

During his half-hour walk home from a brief kiss of goodbye at the end of the street where she lived, and a promise to meet in a few days at the club, he felt a strange disheartenment gnawing underneath the incredible ebullient happiness that carried him along.

133

He saw her little in the next six weeks, and knew from the loud hearsay bandied about that she was going now and again with George Butler, and even that he had 'had it off her'. When more names were mentioned to her fast-maturing credit he was determined not to let grass grow under his feet. The fresh dates he made with other girls carried him further in a week than he'd got in months with her. But it wasn't the same, and he was tormented by her face, her soft voice, and dark hair.

Her smile at him was knowing and friendly, and promised less than when it had been cold and she had wanted him to do all the talking. It was true he was going to Leicester in a few weeks, but he did not see what that had to do with it, for with trains all day he could see her so often she wouldn't know the difference.

She had taken to using lipstick, and her voice had not the same pull-back into her own quiet centre. Her sister didn't come to her aid any more because there was no need to. This made little difference because she had still not become one of the loud and merry talkers, but when she hung back there was more confidence in it, almost as if she did it for a purpose. It seemed now that anybody could take her out, and this included Alec, because when he asked her to come to the café in Pelham Street she agreed.

They sat in a corner of the hushed and modern room, and Mavis said how nice a place it was, and that if ever she got married this was the sort of decoration she wanted for the front room of her house.

Her gaze was drawn by the coloured shade of the lamp whose light fixed itself on her cheeks and the soft coating of make-up she had put there. The faint smell of it drifting across reminded him of the presence of his aunts when they came for a visit as a child. It was disturbing, and he wished she hadn't taken to lipstick and powder because of this faint connection with the dimness of years gone by.

'When do you go?'

'Next week,' he said. 'But I'll come up and see you, you know that.'

'Will you?'

If she had said 'Shall you?' it would have sounded more encouraging. But she didn't, and that was that. He picked up the card: 'Let's have some soup. All right?'

She wore a white blouse with a wide collar, which made her look broader and older. 'If you like.'

'I'll be up to see you, you can bet.' He saw it was a mistake to repeat it, as if he were trying to convince himself, not her.

'When?'

'Next weekend. I've got a job already. The pay's even better than here.'

She folded her paper serviette into triangles, until she couldn't make it any smaller. 'What do they make?'

'Electrical stuff. Same as where I'm at now.'

'I wish I was going away.'

'Where would you go?'

'I don't know,' she said.

He wouldn't come at the weekend, even though she didn't draw her hand away when he reached under the table.

'I might not be in when you come,' she added. 'I might be out. I might not want to see you' – and he wondered why she went on teasing him like this.

'I love you,' he said, blind to everything. 'You know that, don't you?' he meant it, he told himself, and knew it to be more true than anything he'd ever said, which was why it would be so hard to come and see her, in case she wasn't there, as she had threatened.

She took her hand away. 'Are you sure?'

He had a feeling, and hoped he was wrong, and ended up knowing he was wrong, that she had only come out to supper with him because she was making a story from it like that sloppy sort in magazines he'd seen her with. It was something in her eyes that told him this, and the way her lips were about to move but never did when she looked at him. Her head was always slightly turned when she opened her mouth.

After a few days in Leicester he got a note saying she'd like it very much if they never saw each other again.

There wasn't an hour that she was out of his thoughts. He even dreamed about her when he'd hardly ever dreamed in his life before. He talked long hours to her, persuading her to go for a walk, get engaged, marry him, anything to end the torment and start real happiness for the rest of their lives. Happiness began in his dreams when he made love to her.

Going with other girls wasn't the same, and there was less talent to click with because he didn't feel like it. Even when there was they sensed a lack in him, or lost interest because something which gripped at his heart would bode no good for them. He seemed too different, wasn't all there, and so nothing lasted. Not that he wanted it to.

A fair-looking blonde girl with a mole on her neck talked to him at work, and they started going out together. She was nice and pleasant, and open in everything she said, letting him go all the way with her providing he took the trouble to stop her getting pregnant.

He was surprised she could find much to stick with in a person like him, but he was struck most of all by what she said when they were walking back one night from the field they'd been making love in: 'I like you because you don't say much in a loud-mouthed way, like some of the chaps at our place. You talk quiet, and I like that.'

The next day was Saturday and he could stand it no longer. He got on a train for Nottingham.

He took a bus from Midland Station, and changed to another in the town centre, already feeling better at being closer to Mavis. From the top deck he looked at places where they'd walked a year ago – and might again if she felt in any small way for him as he did for her.

In the old days he'd never actually gone to her house and knocked at the door to ask if she was in. He didn't know how she'd take such brashness, but it was the only thing he could do. As he got closer he was afraid of having nothing to say when they came face to face, but she might not be at home anyway, at which he thought of several things, mostly daft and unimportant, but at least he wouldn't be rooted there like a dumb gawk.

The familiar air encouraged him, together with his heart pushing at the inside of his best suit. It would be better to go to the back door so as to cause least disturbance, and she'd get more quickly to that than the front, anyway, so that if the worst happened and she slammed it in his face it would be over quickly. It was pointless wasting time on something that harrowed you so much.

He had an impulse to run, as if the boiling surf of hell were waiting to pull him in. But his legs, more determined than they'd ever been, took him along the entry where he opened the wooden gate with its rusty latch.

His knee-joints seized up in hesitation, then got to work and took him by the coalhouse and lavatory till there was nothing he could do but get a tight hand from his pocket and knock at the door. Even then he thought of going away, until wrenched by the alarming noise of his knuckles tapping a second time on the wood. He noticed how paint was blistering on the middle panel.

It would be better if her sister Helen came to the door, and he started to rephrase his greetings just in case. It might even be one of her parents.

The door opened and Mavis stood before him, leaning towards one of the lintels.

At least it appeared to be her, and he stared a bit too hard for anybody to feel pleased at him suddenly turning up. She wore heels that made her seem taller. 'I thought I'd come to say hello,' he said, 'being in Nottingham a few days.'

She was almost fat, he saw while waiting for an answer, or a formal greeting at least. Her lips and cheeks were heavily made up, and he could smell it where he stood. Arms showed plump from the shortened sleeves of her damson-coloured sweater.

She was looking at him in the hope that he would vanish, a petulant expression on her lips as if wondering why he'd got the cheek to come knocking at her door and imagine she would go out with somebody like him.

'Do you want to come for a drink tonight?' he said.

She must have a regular boyfriend, for the look he was given could mean nothing else. Her eyes seemed to get smaller at the flush of sharp resentment on her cheeks, and he wondered in fact whether there wasn't a youth in the house at this moment with whom she had been about to make love.

He knew she still saw herself as the much-wanted dark beauty of good figure and small stature, and he twigged that because of this she thought he had no right to come pestering her. But to him she had changed so much as to be almost a different person, while she still considered herself to be worth more than him and able to do twenty times better. It was clear that she did not know how much she had altered. It made him sorry for himself, but sorrier for her, which did nothing therefore to damp down his love.

He said to himself, after another quick glance directly into her eyes, that even so, even if she was, though he couldn't be finally sure she was pregnant, he'd keep on going out with her if she was only half-way willing but nevertheless wanted to, and even marry her if she thought it might be a good way out of her trouble.

She broke her silence, and he knew she hadn't sensed anything of what was in his mind. Her world was miles away from him and his. 'I don't want to go out with you.'

He made one last try: 'Can't you?'

'No.'

She closed the door even before he reached the gate.

It gave him something to think about on his way back to the station, to brood on for months afterwards till he forgot her or, to be more truthful, remembered her only as he'd recall a dream, the final blow of it leading to the earlier time when he'd thought she was the first and last and only girl he had been in love with.

When the train was ready to leave he was certain there'd be no chance of her hurrying down the stone steps to call him back and say anything it might do him the least bit good to hear.

He opened his sandwich pack when the train began, and sat back to think about where he'd gone wrong. He considered that twenty-five miles was long enough to do it in – not yet knowing he would never lose that feeling of having loved in vain, and would hardly realise through the years that followed where the strength came from that he grew to need.

Yet a presentiment of this led him to wonder whether everything that had happened to Mavis could be blamed on him, and he decided against it when the pit that opened was too deep and black.

THE CHIKER

'What would you rather have to keep you warm, my little pee-thing, or a new fur coat?' Ken whispered to his girl-friend in the fertile darkness of a double entry.

'Your little pee-thing,' she giggled, which pleased him so much he gave her a fur coat as well.

The trouble was that while he was still paying for the fur coat on hire purchase his little pee-thing gave her a baby, so he had to marry her and be done with it.

If he'd been a few years older she'd have been young enough to be his daughter. He wouldn't have minded, but she wasn't even pretty, and soon looked as old as he was, which served him right for getting carried away in the first place.

He didn't like things to happen so fast. When they did he got angry and wanted to go to sleep. Perhaps that's because he had been twelve years in the army and without a trouble in the world, a time when nothing happened that was his own fault.

Even four years as a prisoner of the Japanese wasn't on his conscience, so it hadn't really happened, except that he knew it had. You could blame the bleeding generals for that. Such people were the same in civvy street or out. The managing director of the firm he worked at had a face similar to the C.O. of his old battalion.

Ken had fought like a mad bastard. In an attack he'd scream louder than the Japs, and couldn't forget the contemptuous look from his platoon commander as they were moving between the rubber trees. The next thing was, *he'd* snuffed it, Ken didn't stop to pick him up or turn to see if he was only wounded.

He remembered sitting by a tree eating the last of his rations, and when a Jap stood over him with fixed bayonet what could he do but offer some? He cracked the butt on top of his head though, and took the lot, which Ken supposed he'd have done in his place anyway.

He lost half his weight and nearly died a few times. Scurvy, beri-beri, and Mongolian footrot chased themselves in and out of his system till his face was so pitted it looked like the front of a Sheffield pikelet.

His teeth went and his hair got thin, but six months back in lovely old Nottingham and he was as right as rain. It's funny how quick you change from good to bad. Other way as well, I dare say. But he never wanted to go through that lot again, knowing there are things in a man's life he can't survive twice. You could tell by his face that he used to be an optimist.

All he had to show for nearly four years was a cigarette lighter taken from a Japanese guard when the war ended. Looting was forbidden by the British officers. It simply wasn't done. You had to leave it for them to do. But he chased the Jap into the bush and beat the living shit out of him to get that lighter. He'd been weak enough at the time, with only a fortnight's good grub in him, but with fists so full of greed and vengeance nothing could stop them.

It was a fine-looking gold-plated titbit, fit to last a lifetime. Even now it was a good igniter, wind or no wind, though he'd had it repaired a few times since.

He was thirty when he came back, and looked fifty. Now he appeared the fifty that he was, a small muscular man with short curly hair that had grown like a miracle as soon as he got home to the land of rain and fog. He worked for a firm that baled waste paper from local factories and sent it off to be repulped. He screwed the press-top as high as it would go, piled in the rammel, and pushed the button that formed it into a compact bale and laced it up with wire. Then he released it from its box, and hauled out as neat a cube as any man could who'd been so long on the job.

So because of his pee-thing twenty years ago he'd had to marry her, and if it hadn't been for his mother dying at the shock of

144

it, or near enough in time for him to think so, they wouldn't have had a house to live in.

He'd craved for his life to settle into a long routine, but the child he married her for had died at birth. Another didn't come for three more years, a girl who was now fifteen, so buxom and sloppy he'd have to keep an eye on her, though she'd already had one boyfriend from what he had seen.

But he was no angel either, and his marriage had been on the run a few times since, when the mutton-dagger dance came at him. Standing by his press at work he thought the only solution was to have it cut off, but then he got to wondering what he'd pee with if it was.

'That's what frightens me,' he said to his mates in the pub, throwing his last dart and missing the double-seven down from three-o-one which would have wiped the floor with them in one deft stroke. 'Otherwise I'd have the bloody thing done tomorrow.'

On a warm evening in June he stood up from the hearth and told his wife not to forget to feed the canary because he was going to the pub for an hour or two.

'Don't get drunk,' she said, 'and try not to be too late. It's work tomorrow. I expect I'll be in bed by the time you get home.'

Such orders satisfied them, because even though everything was dead between them, at least they understood each other. He would be glad of some fresh air, and she to see the back of him till morning.

The collar of his white shirt was spread outside his jacket, and he smoked a cigarette contentedly. Alone and on the loose he felt at peace, as if he'd swallowed a dose of pep-pills young kids talk about.

Girls he passed on the street looked fresh and smart, jolly dollies with lovely joggletits pushing their blouses out, sights that bucked him up so much he felt like singing and not being responsible for his actions. Yet the only thing left for such a runagate as himself if he craved a bit on the side was a juiceless old dawn-plucker for thirty bob who might put the finishing touches on him. It was best to walk the streets and look at it, for all the harm it did.

Fifty if he was a day, he felt fourteen and hoped he looked it to young girls he winked at in passing – but so faintly they might have thought he'd gone a bit rheumy at the eyes and couldn't help himself. Maybe all men of his age felt young enough to be their own sons. What a shame that at fourteen he hadn't realized how they saw themselves as no older than he was then, and didn't know much more about the world.

They only tricked you into thinking they did by putting on a swank about it, wearing their age or grey hairs like the corporal his stripes in the army. Now he was in the same boat and felt as if, on his way up through the orphanage and army, marriage and factory, he'd not been allowed to grow older properly like some people he knew.

It was the best part of the year, a calm summer evening when everybody had stopped work, and time had put its brakes on so that he would live for ever. When you had that feeling what could you do but think of love and let your little pee-thing stir?

One small cloud dented the sky, but on reaching the hilltop at Canning Circus it had gone, as if sucked in by the Trent and blown out to sea. He didn't feel like going into a pub, being held from such human joshing on an evening that seemed too good to waste. Something in his chemical set-up made him already half merry to himself, but it was a faint inebriation caused through a definite lack, and not from having had too much of anything.

People sat around Slab Square, and after a leisurely patrol he went down Wheeler Gate, but not too fast, nor looking into the sky. It was the wrong side of the city to bump into any friends, which seemed a good reason for coming here, then crossing the canal and going on by the station. He thought how good it would be to meet an old flame who would suddenly turn a corner and say: 'Hey up, Kenny, how are you, my duck?' – especially if neither of them had grown a day older.

It wasn't likely. Not widow, wife, or whore with a door to knock on in the whole dead-beat district, nothing to stir the entrails of the heart in this or any other part of town during the last few years.

It was more than that he wanted. It must have been, because he couldn't think what it was. A young chap walked from the bus stop with two suitcases, into the station to take a train somewhere.

He wondered what other town he'd get to, and saw him reaching it in two hours time, a strange place whose streets he didn't know, smelling of bus fumes and dust. He'd get a room at a boarding house and sleep content in a different bed, rising early in the morning to go out and look for a job. Or maybe he had pals where he was going, or his family, or even a girl friend.

He walked faster at such questions since he had no hope of answering them, though he felt happier at speculating on the life of one man who was travelling, for it made the world bigger and more interesting, and he less alone in it. If people could still get on trains there was a chance for him yet, though he knew he would never catch one himself because he didn't need to strongly enough.

He only wanted to go where he was walking, but where that was he didn't know, except that his steps took him to a beer-off with a fading sign painted on a sheet of tin above the door saying: 'CAKES PASTRIES SWEETS AND MINERALS.' During a guarded walk from the orphanage in the olden days such a placard would have made his mouth water, but now it only brought back the memory of his early times.

With a comforting chink of cupro-nickel in his pocket he went in for a packet of cigarettes. The meaty smell of ale and cooked ham reminded him that he hadn't yet supped his nightly pint, but he preferred to wait till it was dark so as to get the full benefit of leaving the shadowy street and entering the lighted guts of a pub.

It was nine o'clock and almost dusk by the time he leaned on the parapet of Trent Bridge. A streak of snake-yellow lay in the western sky, and the river glistened below as if it had a deep black sky of its own.

He'd had a short life so far, even though he'd done so much of it. It had passed him by in big chunks that now seemed no time at all. Every change had been set off by a hidden fuse. When he was three his father left his mother, so she put him into Bulwell Hall orphanage till he was fifteen because she couldn't afford to keep him. Then she brought him out so that he could go to work and earn her some money. A few years later she got into bed with him one morning saying: 'I've loved you ever since you was a baby, Kenny.' The next day he joined the army.

He didn't know why he thought of it now, though it never left him. Other knocks were too recent to be considered. Perhaps they really hadn't mattered all that much, he thought, letting his fag-end drop into the sky below.

He crossed the road and went down a lane along the river bank. A breeze shaking in from the countryside made him feel colder than he'd done all day. His eyes got used to the darkness and he noticed how the twilight was lasting. Away from the river he could make out hedges, and hummocks of grass.

A courting couple lingered by a bush, arms around each other as they moved into one shape. Ken knelt to tie the shoe-lace that had bothered him since leaving the bridge, his eyes level on the two people, a clump of osiers keeping him hidden. The shadow came apart and he squinted as if to bring it closer.

Satisfied that no one was nearby, the man spread his over-coat. 'What are we up to then?' Ken wondered. 'As if I didn't know!' The girl must have sat down also, for they went out of sight for another kiss.

He wanted to clear his throat, but the trundling river some way behind wasn't loud enough to hide the noise he would make. A pint of beer would ease his gullet, but he was too intent on going forward, knees bent, hands splayed as if about to fall on all fours and push himself through the grass as he had once done so skilfully in the Malayan jungle. You don't forget anything, he thought, and that's a fact, wanting to light a cigarette but having to postpone that too till later.

A rustling from close by sounded as if an animal were stirring itself before making up its mind to lumber out and get him. Over the field was a thin white moon when he lifted his head.

The man was on top of the woman, and one of her white legs showed plainly, the almost luminous flesh moving about like a dismembered part of her. They were murmuring as they made love, and he craved to hear what was being said, as much as see what was done, because he never spoke at such times, leaving it to the woman if she felt that way.

He took the lighter from his pocket, to comfort the palm of his hand with a compact and metal object that worked to perfection and asked no questions. It helped to calm him at something he hadn't done since a child when, escaping for an hour from playtime at the orphanage, he had chiked a courting couple in the woods near by.

He felt guilty at chiking, and thought he should go back before the pubs put their towels on. The only sound was one of mutual appreciation going out to the moon. They must love each other, considering how they moaned while at it. He wondered what he sounded like at home, though not being able to chike himself it was something he'd never know.

The lighter rolled in his palm. He wanted to stop it and press the top, see its flame spurt into a yellow shape and glow on the damp grass that was wetting his trousers at the knee-cap.

149

Though it might warm his windbitten face it would give the game away.

They went on longer than him, and didn't complain at the chill. He made up his mind to pull back and go but was fixed in their act and unable to move. His eyes grew large, outweighed his body and rooted him there.

A light drizzle blew across the fields. They ended suddenly and the man stood up. Half-way to his own feet Ken felt the lighter slide from his hand.

He glanced at the couple to make sure they had finished. The man turned but, thinking he was some low bush that had grown while they were making love, or seeing nothing strange because the details of the landscape had failed to impress him while searching for a place to lie down, he turned back to ask the girl if she was all right.

Ken ran his hand through the grass to pick up his lighter. It was time to make his secret retreat. But he didn't want to go. He was happy enough to stay there for ever.

The girl was smoothing her skirt: 'We'll be late.'

Late for what? he wondered, his hand moving quickly to look for his lighter. They were kissing again, in a subdued and tender mood, and he paused in case he might miss something, then hoped they would get down a few more minutes so that he could search for his lighter without being seen.

Extending the area, he lost the exact spot where he supposed he had dropped it. Swearing, he sent his arms in wider circles, half on his feet as if for a better view of what was too dark to see anyway.

He stood up and kicked at the grass he had been lying on, longing to feel its gentle knock against his toecap.

'There's somebody there,' the girl said, in a voice of shame and alarm. 'He's been there all the time,' she wailed. 'Look!'

'Hey you, you bastard,' a gruff voice called, responding to her clear invitation to get him.

Ken would normally have squared whoever named him

such a thing into a similar pulverized shape to that which came out of his press when he had given it the works. But it was raining, and who could be bothered at such a time? Having watched them at their games, he'd rather not show his face – though what could they expect but get looked at if they did it in the open?

There was a rushing of feet through the grass: 'Come 'ere, you dirty bleeding chiker.'

He felt he ought to run, but could not do a thing like that. A grip latched at his elbow, more than any man could bear who was out on a harmless walk before going into a pub for his evening pint. He swung, and caught the man a full hard blow in the stomach.

'Oh Bill!' the girl cried, as if she had felt the pain of it, and now thinking that a chiker might be more dangerous than her boy friend seemed to.

The fact that Ken's solid fist landed where it did, when he had meant it for a higher place, showed how much taller the man was. He had time to wonder not only why he hadn't run when there was still a chance, but why he had strayed by the river at all.

He brooded afterwards. Being taller, the man had the advantage of a longer reach, apart from being half his age. He took Ken by the lapels and lammed into him, not just out of revenge for the first strike which, Ken felt as the stars spun, must have been feeble by comparison, but also because he had moral right on his side at having been disturbed in his sweet evening fuck on the grass.

Ken fell under the vicious hailstorm, and the man stood with fists poised for when he should get up. 'I'll kill you,' he said.

At the feel of wet blood and flesh on fire Ken stayed kneeling, afraid the man might actually try to. 'I was looking for my lighter,' he explained. 'I lost my lighter.'

'Tell me another, you chiker. *You chiker!*' – and he aimed a screaming kick that knocked him flat.

The girl pulled his arm: 'Leave him, Bill. He's just a rotten animal. They can't help it.'

'I ought to throw him in the river.

'Oh shut up, and come on.'

They went away, arguing.

Things were never as bad as they seemed, though the pain told him that they almost were. He stood up when the couple were beyond sight and earshot and walked back to where he had lain. He couldn't find his lighter in a month of Sundays, nor ever recognise the man who had bashed him up. Revenge was out of the question, a desolate sensation.

He smoothed his jacket, glancing around in case the man in his poisonous rage was waiting to paste him once more. But he was alone, and dipped his handkerchief in a pool to wipe his face. Got in a fight in a pub, he said on his way to the bridge. Gave the bastard what-for. I know I'm bruised, but you should see his mangled clock. Lighter? Got my pocket picked. I'll have to get a new one. I was fed up with it, anyway.

Talking thus to his wife, or even his mates at work, he walked into the lights to get the last bus home, feeling far away from any convivial pub.

The usual lamp post didn't shine, because somebody had put its bulb out the night before, but going towards home it felt as if the scalding burn of its filament had been transferred to his own flesh. The window was in darkness, so it seemed everybody was in bed.

From the pavement the front door opened straight into the parlour, and pressing the light-switch he saw Janice lying under her boy friend on the settee. The place stank so much it nearly pushed him back into the street.

They straightened themselves. Janice, expecting him to rant and bawl, was more frightened the longer he kept quiet. Usually so talkative, he held his face at an angle, not wanting to take in what he plainly saw, even though it only heightened the bruises on his cheeks and forehead.

'What's wrong with your face, dad?'

'I saw you,' he cried, his hand brushing her question away as if it were a troublesome fly.

'We was lying down,' said Bernard, a youth who lived a few doors along the street.

'Is that what you call it?'

'What did it look like?'

'Less o' your bloody cheek!' But he hung his jacket on the back of the door with a gesture that took the bite from his words and made Janice think it might yet be all right.

She straightened her skirt: 'I don't see what you've got to shout about.'

'It stinks like a brothel.' He turned to Bernard: 'Get out, you.'

'I was going to make him a cup of tea,' his daughter said.

Ken reached her quickly and the sound of his smack at her face bounced from the four walls right back against him. 'Pick up your pants, you filthy bitch!'

'I'm not a filthy bitch,' she wept, reaching down to the settee.

'Touch her once more, and I'll do you,' Bernard said, though plainly afraid of him.

'Get to bed,' he ordered Janice.

'I'm fifteen,' she cried out at the injustice of life, 'and I go to work. I'm fed up with this.' On seeing his hand move she rushed out of the room and up the stairs.

Bernard was sullen. 'You'd better not do that again.'

'Piss off, you.'

'She'll let me know tomorrow if you do.'

He lit a cigarette from a box of matches on the shelf. The door clicked softly as Bernard left. He'd show 'em. She was too young for it yet, even though she'd had it already. There wasn't much you could do about it if the world was to go on, but at least they could stop using his front room.

Smoke from his cigarette inflated him with a sort of warmth. The good mood he'd started the evening with came back to him, and reminded him of his lost lighter. He sat and brooded on it, and didn't like brooding because it got you nowhere. Anybody knew that, so it was best not to do it, except when you couldn't help it.

The canary woke and made merry, while Ken was black with a grieved sort of worry. It sang as if wound tight by some mysterious force that wouldn't let up no matter how late it was. A piece of his own heart had been ripped away, and he didn't like it: 'For God's sake, stop your noise.'

It might have heard, but took no notice, flitted around its circular cage and went on whistling. Birds had to sing when they were cooped up, though why did it go on without stopping? It was no good putting your hands to your ears because such noise could get through anything. Its beak pointed at him when he stood, opening and closing as if trilling a tune to the four corners of the room in turn.

'Be quiet, you bastard. Knock off.'

He smiled when it stopped, as if obeying him, but suddenly it started again, more full-throated and clogged with life than ever.

A blaze joined his eyes together, packed in with ice at the temples. He set the cage on the rug and, careful to prevent the bird escaping, opened the door and stuffed in crumpled news-paper, one piece after the other till it filled half the cage. The bird sat on top, flitting around in the small space left to con-tinue its endless and piercing song.

He took the firescreen away. The cage fitted the grate as perfectly as his packs of waste paper slotted into the press-jig when he baled them.

Lighting another cigarette, he threw the dead match down. There was no time left. He felt neither young nor old, neither lit up nor black dead, only a cubic area of matter sitting by a cool summer fireplace that had a bird cage in it, from which a concatenating whistle chipped away the last fibres of his organism.

Face set hard with emptiness, he struck a match and held it through the bars of the cage: '*Now* stop it.'

He had a vision of smoke and flame drawn swiftly up the chimney. With a roar and rustle it would put a final stop to the singing. He dropped the match when it burned his finger.

Being alive again, he bent and opened the cage, put his hand in to get the bird again and set it free.

The firescreen fell at his attempts to grasp it, and blood flooded his head from the quick change of position. He sat exhausted in the armchair. The bird stayed where it was, in spite of the door being open, but it didn't sing any more.

A car went by, like a heavy blanket being dragged along the street. Stones weighed at his heart with so much force that it was even more difficult to say what was tormenting him. He exchanged the silence for deep sobs which rent every part of his body.

His wife came downstairs, wondering what it was, softly in case it was nothing. She stood behind the door, breathing slowly so that he shouldn't hear her through his weeping. 'That's twice he's done that in the last year,' she said to herself. 'I'd better leave him alone so's he can get over it.'

She walked slowly up to bed, needing her sleep because she had to get him to work in the morning.

Ken drew the curtains fully back and opened the window on to the street. He looked blankly at the bird and the wide open door of its cage, but it seemed as if it would never make a move.

It sat on its perch and kept quiet, waiting for him to shut it before beginning its song again.

THE END OF ENOCH?

I was asked by the matron of a clinic where I recently had an operation whether I would ever write a sequel to 'Enoch's Two Letters', which she had read in a magazine. She wanted to know, and quite rightly, what finally happened to an eight-year-old boy who had been abandoned by his parents.

At the time I was in no position to consider her request, and now that I am I can only argue in her favour. Perhaps I should have finished the story properly at the time, but I felt then that the important thing was why he was abandoned, and not so much what took place after he was. Yet thinking about it, it seemed quite natural that Miss E——, or indeed anybody else, should want to know more about Enoch. I would also like to know, and so decided to find out for the possible benefit of all concerned.

Of course, this is a story, not a case history, and so it isn't simply a matter of writing a few letters, or going to Nottingham to read the newspaper files, or talking to the neighbours in the street where Enoch stayed with his grandmother. It's not as easy as that.

Nor is it easy to write the end of the story. Even after finishing this one I might be lucky enough to get a letter from some reader, irate or otherwise, asking what happened after that. And then after that. There is rarely an end to any story, only an arbitrary decision by the writer when he's had enough and can't think of anything else to say, or when various demons in the people of the story have temporarily run out of mischief. Or let's say he tries to stop writing when something definite has happened, when the climb down from a big event has landed the main character either in marriage, a mental home, or a state of near-contentment according to the rules and expectations of the society we live in.

The first story about Enoch happened many years ago, and I can bring you up to press (as they say) in a few more pages. Enoch's mother left the house one morning intending never to come back to the husband, and as the demon that held them apart would have it, the father left home on the same day determined not to return to his wife. Each thought that the other (whom they had had enough of, to put it succinctly) would still be there to look after the fruit of their ten-year misalliance – red-haired, round-faced Enoch – when he came home that afternoon from school.

But no one was there, and after staying the long night by himself – poor little boggar, as the neighbours said sympathetically when the story got out – he had the gumption to get on a bus and go to his grandma's house miles away across town.

When his mother reached Hull she wrote to her husband, and when his father arrived in London he dropped a line to his wife – one envelope white and the other blue (as if it made any difference) – and both were picked up by the grandmother when she went back with Enoch the following day. She took Enoch and the letters home with her, and all three items stayed unopened for years, the letters propped behind the walnut-wood biscuit barrel on the sideboard, waiting, like Enoch himself, to be claimed, or sent on when news was heard.

Many a time when Enoch was in bed and she sat by the fire waiting for her forty-year-old son Tom to come back from his surreptitious courting, she picked them up and turned them over. She saw herself opening them, heard the sound of crinkling paper as she unfolded it, to see if any address was inside so that maybe she could put Enoch back in touch with his parents. But a letter was a letter, and neither one was addressed to her. They had stamps on that had been bought with money, and she had no right to touch or read anything that was inside. All she could do was wait until they came back – one or the other of them – so that she could hand them over, together with a piece of her mind, which meant the biggest bloody rollicking they'd ever had in their selfish and unthinking lives.

Whatever they'd done they'd done it for good though, or so it appeared, which was something she helped to make sure of by selling off their furniture and telling the agents that they'd left the house. When she walked past it a few weeks later it was already filled by another family. What bit of money she got for the furniture and belongings bought a secondhand telly and a few clothes for Enoch – at one canny blow providing for his physical and spiritual wellbeing.

She told the Child Welfare when they nosed around that Enoch's parents had farmed him on her 'by prior arrangement'. That was Tom's phrase, and she added, as if only by afterthought, that she hadn't heard from them since they left more than six months ago.

'No,' she repeated firmly, 'I ain't heard a dicky-bird in all that while.' Unwilling to mix things up too much, she did not mention that they had heard from each other, or at least that some attempt had been made at it.

The Child Welfare Officer was no more than a girl, who from her face didn't seem to know much about the world as yet, though no doubt she did on paper. Still, she was given a cup of tea and a chair to sit on. As a result of the visit a few forms drifted through Grandma's life, but seeing that Enoch was obviously well looked after they were happy to let him stay there.

It took Enoch a long time to get used to living at his grandmother's. He'd often been there visiting with his mother, and always liked the trip across town and the fuss his grandmother made, but actually staying for good in the house was strange to him. It was somewhat quieter than if he'd been living with his parents still, and rare enough because nobody ever seemed to quarrel. For this reason time went more slowly and in a dreamier way.

But though the process was a lot softened by his going to a new school, he was all the time looking forward to living at his grandmother's properly, so that it would become like being with his mother. Even after a year such a state seemed a long time coming. He thought that if it hadn't been for Uncle Tom taking him fishing or to the pictures now and again it wouldn't have looked like coming at all.

By the time he'd forgotten about expecting his life to be normal, he stopped thinking about it, so that it more or less became so, except that at certain times of the year it seemed still as if there was something missing.

Tom was like a lighthouse with his guiding principles and care. He had a fad about memory training, and 'cultivating the powers of observation'. He sat by the fire facing Enoch, who was looking hard at him. Tom took several objects out of his pockets – a few coins, a penknife, a watch, a pencil, a cigarette lighter – and put them into a handkerchief without saying a word but making sure that Enoch's big eyes were on every move. Then, at the same time next day, he asked Enoch to write on a piece of paper all that he'd seen go into the handkerchief the evening before. The idea was, he explained, to find out whether he'd observed correctly, and remembered. Enoch passed often and too easily, so Tom gave it up, though he went on inventing other games and wit-tests.

A long time went by until Enoch was ten. One day he wondered sharply to himself when his mother was coming back, and piped up to his grandmother: 'Where do you think my mam is?'

She looked at him hard and a bit long, as if he'd said a dirty word, or farted at Sunday dinner. Then she smiled, and pushed her glasses back up her nose: 'She's gone off with a black man, for all I know. Get over there while I lay the table.'

'What shall I do, then?' he asked.

She opened the knife-and-fork drawer, and put her hands in

without looking: 'You're all right here, aren't you? You're as right as rain, with me and Tom.'

'I know I am,' he said, thinking that was that. There were bushes in the back garden, and a lilac tree, more growing green than there'd been in the house down Radford.

In spring he wondered the same questions as he sat at the table for dinner. Outside, it was sun one minute and snow the next, the greenery either black, or dazzling its way back to emerald. It was the worst spring for a long time, the worst this year, any road up. Only the birds were doing well out of it, having gorged the breakfast scraps. One was so fat that when it swallowed a piece of bread it waddled away like a duck. It just got to a bush before it fell over.

She went out for an hour on business of her own and it seemed as if she'd been gone for years, and that it would take years getting to know her again when she came back. Whenever she walked out of the house, especially in summer, he thought she had gone for ever, and wondered who he'd move on to now.

At times of black frost it was a different matter. You knew how things stood, and could sit by the fire eating bread and best butter. But this time he didn't feel so good because he'd got the hot flushes. Even the television made his head ache, and when his grandma thought as much she switched it off and sat dozing opposite. He not only wondered why his mother had gone, but what he'd done with her. He must have done something with her if she'd gone, and she must have gone because he hadn't seen her for such a long time.

The fact that he'd sold her to a circus played on his mind whenever he thought about it. When the big tall man with a top hat and whip had come to fetch her Enoch had taken the four pounds ten that had been pushed into his hand and gone off to spend it on sweets.

His mother must be roaring in a cage somewhere, though he supposed she'd grown to like it by now, since she didn't think to escape and come back. Maybe she'd even married a lion, you never knew. Anything like that could happen. But he was the one who sold her to a circus, so it was all his fault that she wasn't here no more.

When the man gave him the money he'd winked at him, and squeezed his fingers so hard that his ear began to itch. He remembered it plainly, almost as plain as a dream. And when he scratched his ear to stop it itching, he got the hiccups, and he hiccuped while his mother was being taken out to join the circus he'd wickedly sold her to, and the hiccups didn't properly stop till he stuffed the first sweets into his mouth while still standing in the shop. You had to get something for doing a thing like that to your mother. He hoped she'd done well at the circus, otherwise the man might turn up and snarl for his money back, saying she was no good to them. If she came back as well he'd have to sell her to another one, to get more sweets.

'You look as if you're ready for a talk with the chimney-sweep,' his grandmother would say to him, after a supper of cocoa and bread-and-cheese, meaning that he should go to bed and get some sleep.

In summer-time he rarely thought about his mother. His grandma asked him to carry a chair into the garden, on a sunny day when it was warm and humid, so that she could sit there and read the paper. When she got tired of that she went into the house for the scissors, then sat on the chair cutting her toenails, while he stayed inside feeling shy about it and doing his homework.

He thought that if she went on cutting her toe-nails like that in the garden, with the hard bits flying all over the grass, maybe a tree would grow in a few years time. What sort of tree though was beyond him to say. But he knew that any sort of tree would be a miracle.

Three years after his mother left, she came back. The time had been very short to her, so little had happened in it. When Enoch grew up and looked back it seemed a very short time to him as well, until he began to think about it, when it became longer and longer, almost as long as it had been at the time.

He only thought properly about it after his grandmother had died. His own mother is still alive, because she married another man and Enoch, who didn't care one way or the other because he spent much time at his grandma's till she died, grew up and got to university, and never regretted the burning fact that he had started it all off by selling his mother to a circus. In any case, she must have had a good time in it, though it hadn't stopped her growing old, nor, at last, coming back to search him out and say nothing at all when she looked at him about what he'd done to her.

His father also came back to Nottingham, and lived with his fancy woman. Enoch saw him from time to time with his other new kids, and was occasionally taken for a treat up Colwick, and even sent something at Christmas and birthdays, though Enoch never forgave him, not until he grew up and realized that nothing that anybody did was their fault, since you were always liable to do the same yourself.

The two letters that his grandmother had saved finally got to where they should have gone a long time ago, but didn't make much difference to Enoch. He saw his mother tear up the one to her from his father into little pieces after hardly reading it. And what his father did with hers he never knew, and forgot to even wonder about.

Enoch only knew that when nothing was happening, everything was happening. The action was only mime. He knew as well that by doing nothing we all connive in our own disasters. One letter would have been enough, if it had been addressed to him – who alone knew what had caused the whole thing.

SCENES FROM THE LIFE OF MARGARET

The budgerigar greeted her as she came in and laid her basket down. The kids ate at school but she needed a meal herself, so took off her coat and lit the gas. Rain swept over fences and clattered against the window as if spring would never cease, she thought, hoping one day for sunshine.

A year ago the bird had got out of his cage and flown into the fire, and though Michael was there to dart in a hand and pull him free, the smell of singed feathers and burned skin was everywhere, and the poor bird lay for days doctored on warm milk and coddled in clean handkerchiefs. Bit by bit it came to life, its warm breast throbbing with song after song, and half-speech imitations that she and the kids had taught him before the accident.

His feathers had grown back in places, vivid emerald and blue, with a patch of white over the left eye. She'd never expected it to live, and found it surprising what fire and grief and God knew what else such a creature could survive. It didn't seem much to do with its own will whether it got back to life or not, but something else which neither of them knew about.

Such reminiscing reminded her of her father's death the year before, and she wondered whether it had been any worse to him than the fire the bird flew into. She'd been afraid to walk into the other ground-floor room and see him, though he was beyond all help and wouldn't have known her. She was too proud of him to see him die, and didn't want to witness what he might in after-life (if there was such a thing, but you never knew) feel ashamed that she had seen.

She mashed some tea, then ate bread and cheese. It was strange how lonely you could be with three strong kids, for they went out hand in hand after breakfast, and didn't roar in again till tea-time. The budgerigar woke from its perch of sleep near the window and sent a trill of stone-chipping notes through its wire cage.

She put in a hand and held the warm soft-feathered body, now singing out its second life as if nothing terrible had ever happened to it. Michael, who was eight at the time, willed it to get through the tunnel of that suffering, while she had given it up. Only the children's tears had brought her faith that it might choose to live after all.

When she opened the cage it darted like a blue pebble over the settee and settled near the front window. For a while they hadn't let it out when the fire was lit. Not that it would have gone there anyway, but it had become too precious for such rash chances. Nowadays it was safer because the chimney was closed, and a less harmful mock-electric fire fitted in the grate.

Carefully closing the door she walked down the path to meet the baker's van. The grey house-roofs were drying, and the freshening air reminded her how some neighbours even grumbled because the estate wasn't so black and cosy as the slum they'd not long left.

One of the eight kids who lived across the road came to buy two loaves. The baker held one hand out to get the money, and the other with the bread, but the child didn't have money to give so he put the bread back.

'I suppose his dad sent him out to try it on,' Margaret laughed, collecting her own loaves.

When he was ready to drive off the kid came again, this time with coins, so that he got the bread. Then three other kids ran from the same house to buy cakes with equally ready cash.

'You'd be surprised at some of the antics people get up to,' the roundsman said, 'just to save a couple o' bob.'

Being on National Assistance and her husband's allowance, money was short for her as well, but they still weren't as bad off as in the old days because she had a council house for one thing, and for another the rest of the family helped her along. Her mother worked at a food warehouse and brought a load of purloined groceries up on the bus every weekend. Her sister was in a shoe factory, so they never had wet feet. Her brother served at a clothing shop and rigged them out when he could. Another was a radio mechanic, so she had a reject telly in the living room. A cousin who helped in a butcher's shop did his best not to forget her.

Now and then she could swap shoes and food and clothes with somebody in the next avenue who worked at a toy depot, or she'd barter with the woman next door who packed up pots and pans for a mail order firm. Her aunt was an overlooker at a tobacco factory and Margaret, not smoking herself, was able to give pilfered fags to a man who dug her garden and occasionally whitewashed the kitchen. What was life worth if you couldn't help each other? The bird flew back to the top of its cage and whistled its agreement from there.

A radio voice talked about a leper colony in Africa, so she switched it to light music. A blue stream of soap powder spun into boiling water and she stirred at the bubbles with a huge wooden spoon that Edie across the way had brought her as a present from Majorca: 'You can use it to bash the kids with when they chelp you,' she laughed.

'Not mine, duck,' Margaret said, standing by the hole in the fence that connected the two houses. 'They do as I tell 'em without that. My kids have to be good, not having any dad. Sometimes I tell myself he don't know the joy he's missing.'

Fifty bright round faces shifted among the bubbles, rainbows breaking in the steam. 'They'll see you right,' Edie said, 'when they go to work. You'll have your joy of 'em yet.'

'They'll get married then, duck,' Margaret prophesied soberly. 'I'll find another man, maybe, when I've got 'em off my hands.'

'I shouldn't wait too long if I was you,' Edie said. 'You're still young. Get a bit of it back up you before you're too old to feel it.'

It made Margaret laugh just to look at her sallow and serious face with its glasses and long false teeth to match, every second waiting for her to say something foul and funny. She didn't know how Edie's husband put up with it yet he seemed to like her well enough.

'I can do without that for a while,' Margaret told her. 'I keep myself company in bed at night, I do' – which sent Edie cackling back to her kitchen It was good to laugh, even if it did show a bad tooth or two. The only chance she got was when they showed old silent comedies on the telly, which she'd look at all night if they was on.

She thought maybe Edie was right, because if somebody was found it wouldn't do to turn him down. Life was too short, but the trouble with men was that they're just like women, she reflected, no better and no worse. And who'd want to take anybody on who's got three kids already? It'd be a rope around his neck right enough, though she'd heard people say there were men who didn't want the bother of a woman having babies, and would rather step into a brood of kids ready-made or half grown up.

But if that was the case where did the woman come in? Maybe he treated her as one of the kids, a pat on the head now and again for good measure. It was surprising what you might end up doing for the kids' sake, if you didn't watch yourself, though if mine don't have a father it's no more than a lot of others have to put up with. Still, it does touch my heart when I ask in the tally-man or window-cleaner for a cup of tea and see them jumping all over his legs.

Men aren't the be-all and end-all of my life, she thought, taking the long prop and wedging the line high, all signals hoisted. Pants, vests, stockings, and socks straightened and flapped in the uprising wind. The less you want something the more likely it is to take place, and the more you picture it, the less chance of it becoming real. What you never imagined were the bad things that hit you, and what you always thought of were the good things that never did.

She had got over her husband leaving her. She had been too shattered and upset by it not to survive.

The sallow catkins were full of yellow dust. It was good to go up the Grove for an afternoon walk, smell the spring water of the Trent flooding by down the steep bank. There was nothing else to do but laugh, except cry, she smiled.

With three kids to be fed and looked after there'd been no time to brood herself into the grave or Mapperly Asylum. There was some justice in the world, though you only thought so when it kicked you in the chops, or hoped so when it was about to. In his rough and cunning fashion he'd made certain she'd never be able to take up with anyone else, though maybe in one sense it was generous of him to leave her the kids, otherwise she might not have got over it.

He and his 'fancy woman' had prospered after opening a corner shop to sell new and second-hand bicycles. He bought old ones at scrap prices and tarted them up in his clever way, while *she* looked after the book-keeping and window-dressing. Margaret met his mother one day in Slab Square, and was told all about it.

It didn't even hurt any more to brood on it, though a man who could forget his children so absolutely must be a real blackguard. He might stop living with his wife, but if he went on loving his kids she could at least console herself that some of this contained a bit of hidden regard for her as well. He never saw them or wrote, nor sent Christmas presents, but had rubbed them out of his life. She sat on a broken elm trunk to rest, wondering how she of all people had ever met such a man.

She thought of the man who courted her before him, as if that might give some clue to it. The war had been on for a long time, though everyone knew it was coming towards its end. Margaret was sixteen, and after two years working in a food factory she joined the Women's Land Army so as to get away from home and 'see life'. All she saw were bulls' heads and pigs' arses, glowering woods and wet fields, and a poky room in a mildewed and leaking cottage which she shared with six other girls, a muddy and sweating life which paid thirty bob a week and a rough sort of keep.

She began to feel like a slave-labouring appendage to the animals, till one of the farmer's men taught her to drive a tractor. She learned quickly and got a licence, but because things were now so much better she was able to look back on how bad they had been, and in a fit of anger that she should have been so much put upon, packed her things one Saturday and walked to the village bus stop. Reaching Nottingham in two hours, she left her case at home and went down Slab Square to see which of her girl friends were in any of the pubs.

After the cold black-out night, bruised by huddled gangs of soldiers, the Eight Bells was like a secret cave cut into the hillside of the street-cliff.

She bought a shandy and, every seat being taken, stood near the bar. An American soldier put his hand on the arm of a girl near by, who shrugged it away:

'Get your hands off me, Yank!'

'Sorry, sister.'

'I'm not your sister.'

'All right, baby.'

'I'm not your bloody baby, either. If you don't lay off I'll part your hair with this pint jar.'

Margaret knew the voice, and saw the face. Smoke and beer-smells, breath and pungent boot-dust exhilarated her. The backs and faces set colourfully along each line of mirrors after two years in the rural dullness heightened the flush in her face and made her stretched limbs tingle.

She laughed at the raucous rat-crack of the protesting voice, knowing it to come from one of her cousins. 'That's right,' she called over. 'You tell him, Eileen.'

The snow-white hair of a suicide-blonde flashed around: 'Hey up, Margaret!'

'I could tell you a mile off,' she said.

'What are yo' doin' 'ere? Up to no good, like me?'

She wished she hadn't spoken, for Eileen's reputation, even in her own family, was almost as low as you could get, her back-chat to the American being only another form of come-on, so that she smiled at him before edging over to Margaret: 'I had a nobble on an hour ago,' she said, apologizing for her lack of success so far, 'but the poor bogger went out to be sick and I ain't seen 'im since. When did you get back from the cow sheds?'

'An hour ago.'

'I'd pack it in, if I was yo'.'

'I did do.'

'About time.' Eileen's thin face stood out from the robust puffiness of the soldiers around. 'I don't blame you. Come and do a stint at the gun factory. You'll never look back. Too much going on up front!'

Margaret's laugh attracted someone she could not see during her talk about old times with Eileen. He told her afterwards how that vital and homely sound had gone right into his heart at a time when he met so much falsity night after night – whether he stayed in camp or not, which he usually did in order to write long letters to his parents back home.

And looking towards her laugh he'd seen someone who hadn't been there before, noting her long dark hair and the pink skin of her plump face. Every young girl was pretty, he admitted, especially if you'd parachuted in with the first wave of the invasion and had the total support of your friends scythed away in a few insane minutes, but *her* face was different, had a refined trust that, after her laugh, and while she was listening to her blonde friend, had a kind of profound and gentle helplessness. It was as if she'd come into the pub, he said, to wait for him as he had been waiting for her ever since getting to England.

He pushed his fresh yet strangely troubled face between

Margaret and her cousin, buying a round for them just before closing time. She could not, even now, gainsay the fact that she was the reason for the drinks. Jimmy Chadburn seemed honest and fair of feature, except for the knife-scar caught in some tussle with a German during the Normandy landings which had closed the left side of his face up a bit. But the right and best side was turned to her, and his inside soul seemed generous enough.

He treated her courteously, and always with a smile, dusted the chair before she sat down, opened the door and prevented her from being jostled as they went out. His teeth were so clean when he smiled that she might have known she couldn't trust him. And it was difficult to tell whether he was lonely or not – as one ought to be able to do with Americans who had so much money.

Large white single clouds passed swiftly through the sky, crossing the broad avenue of trees. She had sat down too long and the damp was pressing in. Tea-time would come and the kids would be home. There was no way or wish to stop the wheel turning day after day and week after week. But she dwelt a little longer on Jimmy Chadburn. He was her first love, yet she'd heard it said that whenever you start thinking of your first love you are about to meet somebody else. Well, she could wait, especially when it was a question of having to.

She kept no mementoes in life, except memory. All letters and photos were burned, and nothing of him remained. He had gone back to the wife he said he didn't have, and left her to nurse herself through the scorching deserts of betrayal and smashed love. How could anyone do such a thing to anyone else?

She supposed it was something all people had to put up with at one time or another. It was hard to think of anybody who hadn't. It was like a vaccination to stop smallpox eating you into a cancer.

The worst thing about being jilted was in the man you took up with afterwards. You acted joyfully because you thought it was all over, not knowing that this was the final bitter kick of it. She saw how true it was now, even though she kept herself free for two years, because it took that long to get over it, which seemed like no time at all when looking back.

It was good to get the ache out of her legs. She broke off a new and living bud, shredded its stickiness with a sharp fingernail, and could hardly remember where she'd met her husband, something that doesn't speak well for any man, almost proving you were never in love with him. Meeting Albert was probably the last flicker indeed of love for Jimmy Chadburn. Some people don't believe in love, which only means they'd never suffered from it. Yet if they hadn't she supposed they were lucky.

She reflected how Albert loved to make her cry, did everything to do so. It was never difficult, but he couldn't stand it when he succeeded, so jeered to make her stop. Walking down the street she slipped on a piece of rotten pavement, and he hit her, adding insult to injury in his usual way. He used to say all's fair in love and war, but she remembered that life itself was war to him, a war to get exactly what he wanted for himself. You had to be careful not to get in the way of what he wanted.

Asking herself what she'd done wrong to make him like this, it became obvious that she was only guilty of having married him – though by then it was too late. In any case he had an equal share of responsibility in having married her. No one could deny it. But to please him she'd have to go out one day and vanish, so that he wouldn't even have the bother of a funeral, though she didn't see why she should be the one to do it and make things easy for him.

After three years and three kids he left her, as she told Edie, 'without even a piece of bread between my lips'. That was the end of that, and as for mementoes, she'd burned even the memories inside herself, stamped on them whenever they threatened to come up, till they hardly ever did any more.

Roy John Callender was an exhibition diver and champion swimmer, whose name was occasionally seen in the more obscure columns of Nottingham newspapers. Though his exhibitions weren't so enthralling, nor his championships so spectacular, he was considered a man of fair showmanship and prowess in local terms, and all who had seen him dive agreed, over their sedentary drink of beer, that at thirty he was in his prime.

'When you cut into the water like a javelin,' he said to Margaret one night in the Maid of Trent, 'and go right down, you think you're dying because it don't seem possible you'll ever get up to fresh air and see daylight again. But you do. Dead right, you do. You don't want to move your arms, like they're tied up with ten balls of string, but they move by themselves and steer you level. Then they push you up, and when your head shoots out of the water you want to go up and up till you crack your noddle on the clouds.'

'Why do you do it, though?' she asked naïvely, even after this description which he had perfected over the years, and which half the people in the pub turned round to listen to.

He laughed fit to die, she thought, and told her when he could get his breath from it: 'I just like the water, I suppose!'

Several times in his career he had dived off Trent Bridge into a canvas area below. Dressed in a one-piece black costume he climbed on to the parapet and, after mock-gymnastics to loosen his limbs in the sharp summer breeze, he faced the chosen crowd with both hands clasped in the air. His stern expression, at the point of turning to begin his dive, changed to a grin of expected success.

Motorists leaned out of their car windows, and lorry drivers waved and wished him luck above the noise of their engines. The black and pink figure framed against the white sky of the distant war memorial turned a somersault above the bridge wall – then fell through the air towards the canvas area of bottle-green water.

He loved doing it, he told Margaret in the pub, because when he made that first great leap he thought he hadn't strength to do it properly, that he would smash himself against the dark stone of the bridge. But he managed it, and the feeling of dropping down so effortlessly and with such spot-on aim was the best in the world, except the sweet dreams that came after going to bed with a woman he loved – he winked.

She suspected him of piling it on a bit. But then, all men did that. He certainly looked a liar as he swaggered in and walked to the bar for his first drink of the evening. Tall and well built, he had a sharp pink face and dark hair receding in a vee back from his forehead.

He was no empty loud-mouth however, for he had done all he told her about, and spoke sincerely enough, though when Margaret questioned Edie as to whether or not she had ever heard of a champion swimmer called Johnny Callender Edie said she hadn't, but that that didn't mean much because she'd never heard of anything, anyway. So Margaret let the promise of him drop, her notion being reinforced that men were bigger bragging liars when they had something to brag about than when they hadn't. It was better to expect nothing so as not to be disappointed.

One afternoon a dark green van drew to the kerb outside the front gate and Callender himself came up the path with a television set in his arms. She met him at the door, flustered and laughing. 'Did you get that from under the water on one of your dives?'

He set it on the kitchen table, loosened his white scarf and unbuttoned his dark three-quarter overcoat. 'It's for you, missis. Or can I call you Margaret?'

'If you've brought that for me, you can. Shall I mash you a

cup of tea?'

'It'll tek the sweat off me.'

'Sit down, then. What sort is it?' She dropped the kettle-lid, and bent to pick it up.

'A good one, don't worry. Brand new.'

'I'll bet it is.'

'No damaged goods where I come from,' he grinned, 'except me, perhaps.'

'You don't want to say that about yourself,' she said, with such seriousness and concern for the safety of his good name that he laughed out loud.

'What's bleddy funny about it, then?' she demanded, cut to the middle. She didn't like being made fun of just because she'd thought his phrase weightier than he could ever have done. 'If that's the way it is you can take your rammel and get out.'

'You don't think I mean it when I run myself down, do you?' he said, tears almost lighting up his deep brown eyes. 'Oh dear, love, when were you born?'

Having been out of circulation for the last nine years there was no telling when she was born, she told him. 'Though it might not have been all that long after you,' she added, 'so don't think yourself so smart.'

The tea-cosy was on the pot for five minutes till it mashed into a mellow brew, but then she poured it sharply as if to get rid of him as soon as possible. The bird warbled from its cage, and he promised next time to bring a budgie because it sounded as if it wanted a mate as well – helping himself to several spoons of sugar. He takes a lot of sweetening, she thought, and maybe he needs stirring up as well, or perhaps I do, though he's not the one to do it, swimmer or not.

'Boy or girl?' he asked, looking up, smile gone.

'Male,' she said, 'and it sings like a man as well. Men allus sing better than women, especially when they want summat. All a woman need do is bide her time. Then what she gets is twice as bad, I suppose.'

180

He sipped his tea as if she might have put a dash of ground glass in it. 'You sound proper old-fashioned.'

'That's nowt to what I *feel*.'

'Why don't you have a cup of tea as well, duck?' he said. 'I'm feeling a bit left out.'

'I was going to,' she said, beginning to like him again.

'Thought I'd get company after what I'd brought,' he reminded her.

It looked so much better than the cronky old set her brother had palmed her off with. 'Are you leaving it?'

'On approval. Depends whether you take to it.'

'Would you like some biscuits?'

'If there's cream in 'em.'

'I can tell you've been at tea with millionaires. It's plain biscuits at this house. If I got cream biscuits they'd go in a second.'

'Kids are like that,' he said, and she wondered if he'd got any of his own.

'Are you going to plug it in for me?'

He dipped a biscuit in his tea, and held it there too long so that most of it fell off. 'If I leave it, I'll have to.'

'It looks like it, don't it?'

The scalding tea went down his throat in one long gulp. 'Let's see to it, then.' He clattered the cup back to its saucer, and they went into the living room together.

He didn't move in, which she thought he might try in his brash fashion, but came to see her once or twice a week, and slept there. He was lavish in presents for the kids, though she saw as plain as day he didn't really like them, and that his generosity didn't come natural to him. He was uneasy under the weight of the kids when in their open good nature they clambered up as if to suck him dry. When Rachel wanted a bedtime story he almost snapped at the second asking. Margaret began to suspect he was married and had kids of his own, but when she tackled him about it he told her he was divorced.

'Why did you tell me you was single, then?'

They sat in a corner of the pub on Saturday night, and in spite of the noise that encapsulated them she almost hissed her question. He looked at her openly, as if proud of what he had done. 'I thought so much of you I didn't want you to think I was secondhand.'

She felt herself blushing. 'I'm the one who's secondhand, so I don't know what you've got to worry about.'

'That's different,' he said. 'I'm the one that's in love with you. If it was the other way round I wouldn't bother so much.'

'I don't know what to think.' She was bewildered at his calculated lies because she did not know how to let on she knew he was lying. His face deepened into seriousness, as if to disarm her even more, until she began to believe in him to such an extent that she wondered whether he wasn't about to ask her to marry him. He suddenly broke this intense silence by laughing out loud and calling the waiter to bring another pint for himself and a short for her.

Her disappointment at this breakage of their closeness increased even more because she did not know which of them was the cause of it. Another opportunity might not come around for weeks, and she didn't feel sure enough of herself to get it back on her own.

His face was such as held its own with the world, so you'd do well to look out for it putting one over on you, she thought, because like all men he treated you as part of the world as well. His face was a hard one, in spite of the gloss that came on it when he wanted something, yet she felt there was a soft centre somewhere – like in the tastiest chocolates.

She prayed for this to be true, because after they'd known each other a few months it was certain beyond all truth she was pregnant.

There was nobody she could spill it to but Edie. Her instinct told her that to let him know the news would drive him away clean and clear, which she didn't want to do, for though she'd started off being wary she now liked him enough to want him with her for good, if only he'd ever grow up and set his selfish mind to it.

The last thing she expected was to bring another kid into the world, but since one was indisputably on its way and might prove impossible to stop she ought to try and get used to the idea – not doubting for a moment that he'd help her all he could, and maybe actually marry her if nothing worked.

There was no point thinking yourself into a black sweat, so she went into the kitchen and put the kettle on for coffee. If she confided her trouble to Edie she might be able to tell her how and where to get rid of it. Certainly, she knew nobody else who would. She fancied there wasn't much Edie didn't know about a thing like that, though having an abortion had never been much in Margaret's mind when she got pregnant. But this time it was different, and nobody could tell her what to do with her own life and body. Three were enough kids in one woman's life, especially now they were getting on and the worst might soon be over.

When Edie pulled the chair from under the table to sit on, and sighed as if she had all the work in the world to do in the small space of her own house, and should never have left it for a moment, it was obvious she had something to tell Margaret, who therefore thought it friendly and polite to let her get it off her chest before coming out with her own worries. In any case, she welcomed a reason to defer it as long as possible.

'How many?' she said, reaching for the bag of sugar. 'What bleddy weather, in't it?'

'Four, Meg,' said Edie. 'Enough to turn you into a fish. Have you seen owt o' that chap o' yours lately?'

'He showed his face a week ago,' said Margaret, thinking it

funny that Edie should mention him when he was on the tip of her own tongue.

'Is he married?'

Margaret thought it an outlandish question, and wondered what was coming.

'I hope you don't mind me asking.' said Edie.

'That's all right, duck. He ain't as far as I know.'

'I saw him in town yesterday, as large as life, with a woman and two kids trailing out of one o' them cheap clothes shops down Hockley. I'm not sure they was his kids, though it looked like it to me. I don't want to be nosy, but I thought you might like to know. The woman looked so miserable she must a bin his wife.'

She stirred Edie's coffee and pushed it towards her, thinking yes it was his sister because he'd mentioned her a few times, till another explanation came to her and she realized she was only making excuses for him. There could be no doubt he was married, because it fitted in with his actions ever since she'd known him. 'Thanks for telling me,' she said, drinking coffee to stop her lips trembling. 'I might have known.'

'They're all the same,' Edie said. 'It don't matter that much.'

'No,' Margaret said, 'it bleddy-well don't, I suppose. It ain't that I mind about him being married. But he might have told me. I hate sly and deceitful people. I expect he was frightened I wouldn't want him if he said he was married.'

'It's no use crying over it, duck,' said Edie, trying to comfort her, and cursing herself for a big-mouth when it suddenly came to her how things stood. 'We bloody women get all the bother, and the men go scot-free.'

Margaret's face was dry and stony: 'Nobody goes scot-free in the end,' she said.

And she didn't ask Edie how to get rid of it, because she felt too much of a fool to let her know she was pregnant.

The hot and fine summer seemed to make it worse. She waited

night after night, and even went to where he said he'd worked, but that was a lie too, for he wasn't there and never had been.

He didn't come for a month, so by the time she told him even her morning sickness was beginning to ease off. When he made an excuse to leave that same evening without going to bed with her, and saying he'd come back again when he'd thought what to do about it, she knew she wouldn't see him any more, but didn't want to make too much fuss in case it turned out not to be true and he came back after all. She laid the kids' things out for school and breakfast, her lips still wet from his one kiss. I shan't die, she thought, and I shan't starve, and neither will the kid I'll have.

What she would do, she thought one tea-time while seeing to the budgerigar, was wait till he next did a bit of exhibition diving at Trent Bridge, and then when he was about to jump she'd burst out of the crowd and run to him, shouting at the top of her voice that he was a rotten no-good get who'd got her pregnant and then run away and left her. Yes, she would. She'd hang on to him and go down into the water and never let go till they both drowned and were out of it for good. Let them put that in the Evening Post so that his wife could read about it while waiting for him to come home after boozing with his pals or from doing another woman. But maybe he'd led his wife a worse dance than he'd led me, and I'm well off without him in spite of having another one to feed and fend for.

The bird flew around the room while she cleaned out its cage. At the sound of seed spilling into its pot it darted back and rested a moment on her hand. 'Hello, my duck,' she said, knowing she'd do nothing of the sort, and not tackle Callender at Trent Bridge, 'you got over your little accident in the fire, didn't you?' – though not sure whether *she* would this time, as tears followed the too bright smile at her eyes.

She shut the door when it began to eat.

In the café, an old man sitting next to her began making funny noises.

He wore a hat and scarf and overcoat, so he wasn't even poor. But he was very old, in spite of a moustache and full head of white vigorous hair. She'd never seen him before, but it seemed nobody else had either, because they weren't disturbed by the noise he was making.

It wasn't loud, and didn't frighten her. She supposed that was why other people weren't bothered. But it was funny, somehow, though she knew it wasn't funny to him because who would feel happy with a noise like that for company – especially an old man who must be pushing eighty?

It wouldn't do to interfere, whatever happened. Maybe he was warming up for a little tiddly-song to himself. Old men were like that, and harmless as long as they weren't dirty as well. But on a bus once when she was twelve an old man put his hand on her knee. There's one thing to be said for an old woman: she wouldn't do a thing like that. So she knocked it away, without causing any fuss.

But if it came back she'd shout at the top of her voice: 'Get your hands off me, you dirty old swine.' Maybe he guessed what was on her mind, since he got up and shuffled out at the next stop. Perhaps he only wanted to tell her something, or was in need of company, or he was about to say she reminded him of his own daughter he hadn't seen for thirty years, not since she was a girl like her. Still, you had to look after yourself, even though she did feel a bit sorry for him.

Her tea was getting cold, but that wasn't the old man's fault, because he couldn't help the noise he was making. It sounded less and less that sort of noise the more it went on. She was the only one with ears. Or maybe the others hadn't washed theirs out that morning.

They sat with tea and buns, set in their newspapers, or staring into the air which must have been more interesting because they didn't even need print to hold them down. If you look into the air you look at yourself, and that must be better than any newspaper.

The old man was too busy with his tiddly-song to take much in. At the sound of such noise his eyes must have stopped looking at anything. Nobody else seemed to understand that his eyes had come to a dead end, for the few who glanced at him turned away as if they had seen nothing. Some talked together, and didn't even bother to look, though they knew what was going on right enough.

It made her uneasy, being by herself. He sat up straight as a soldier against the wall, a hand on the table beside his cup. By making such a noise he was trying to get in touch with some-one, but he did not know who or where they were, which she supposed was why no one could bear to look at him in case it was them. It became more insistent until, to her, it appeared to fill the whole café.

She didn't find the noise meaningless or dispiriting, for it set her memory racing thirty years back to being a child and fading into sleep. Then, as now, she never went from the conscious world straight into sleep like maybe a healthy person would, but into another world between her and deep sleep itself, always a different place through which she had to pass before reaching real sleep, and she only knew she'd done that when she woke up.

She remembered feeling, once in this twilight zone, the horror of being about to die. A huge leaden sphere pressed against her brain as if to crush all five senses at once. As big as the earth, it rolled on to her, till her eyes saw only grey matter and her breath was starting not to pump. She called for her father, who came in and brought her back to full breath by some kind and trivial act of distinction.

Because of this outcome it was not a bad memory that the old man's noise had set off, yet now it began to annoy her, for she had come into the café for a cup of tea as a break from the grind of buying scarves for the children, and hadn't been in five minutes before bumping into this.

An older woman sitting on the other side had wire glasses and straw-blonde hair, and puffed a fag while looking out of the window as if to burn her way through the glass with the acetylene smoke of it. She was nearer, but Margaret couldn't imagine her being bothered by him in a hundred years – till she had the strange idea that maybe everybody else in the café had their heads filled with the same thoughts and words that she had.

Her laugh at this interrupted the noise coming from the man's mouth, her face turning red with shame because he must have heard her and imagined she was laughing at him. She was almost relieved when the rattle started again.

His tie-knot was slightly below the join of the collar. A hand was limp by his side, while the other jerked at the half-empty cup. She thought it a pity he'd let the tea inside get cold, then leaped up and opened his coat, trembling with embarrassment at her big belly getting in the way but acting as if it was the only thing left to do in her life: 'Are you all right? What is it then? Tell me, for God's sake?'

He wanted help, and she wanted help in order to help him, for her voice wavered at his eyes rolling, and the sound of finger nails scraping on tin coming from his clenched lips, pressed tight as if trying to stop something getting out for the last time. She was frightened at the sight of his convulsed body.

She pulled down the knot of his tie and flung it open, snapped his collar at the stud though it wasn't in any way tight at his withered neck: 'Where do you live, duck?'

Trouser-legs chafed at the supports of the table, as if they could stop him falling down to earth, because the bench he sat on was not enough. She looked from the double-white world of his pot-eyes and shouted in a panic: 'Can't somebody give me a hand, then?'

A waitress came over, more, Margaret reflected later,

because she thought I might start to give birth if she didn't, than to be of much use to the old man. 'Is he badly?'

The noise stopped, and he was dead.

'You'd better call an ambulance,' Margaret said, 'and a copper. But he's still more alive though than you bleddy lot in here.'

STAR BOOKS

are available through all good booksellers but, where difficulty is encountered, titles can usually be obtained *by post* from:

Star Book Service,
G.P.O. Box 29,
Douglas,
Isle of Man,
British Isles.

1 or 2 books – retail price + 5p. each copy
3 or more books – retail price post free.

Customers outside Britain should include 7p. postage and packing for every book ordered.